"MOVE AND I'LL DRILL YOU," SLOCUM CALLED, WONDERING WHAT REACTION HE'D GET.

He was not expecting the gunshot that tore through the darkness to the left of his ear. Ducking instinctively saved him from the second slug that would have blown off his head.

He hit the ground, grunted and got his six-gun out. Rather than firing blindly, he waited for a decent target. A foot-long tongue of flame licked in his direction as the unseen man fired yet again.

Slocum lined up his barrel and shot. He was rewarded with a sudden, final yelp in the darkness.

DON'T MISS THESE
ALL-ACTION WESTERN SERIES
FROM THE BERKLEY PUBLISHING GROUP

THE GUNSMITH by J. R. Roberts
Clint Adams was a legend among lawmen, outlaws, and ladies. They called him . . . the Gunsmith.

LONGARM by Tabor Evans
The popular long-running series about U.S. Deputy Marshal Long—his life, his loves, his fight for justice.

SLOCUM by Jake Logan
Today's longest-running action Western. John Slocum rides a deadly trail of hot blood and cold steel.

BUSHWHACKERS by B. J. Lanagan
An action-packed series by the creators of Longarm! The rousing adventures of the most brutal gang of cutthroats ever assembled—Quantrill's Raiders.

JAKE LOGAN

SLOCUM AND THE GREAT DIAMOND HOAX

J

JOVE BOOKS, NEW YORK

SLOCUM AND THE GREAT DIAMOND HOAX

A Jove Book / published by arrangement with
the author

PRINTING HISTORY
Jove edition / July 1998

The Penguin Putnam Inc. World Wide Web site address is
http://www.penguinputnam.com

ISBN: 0-515-12301-3

A JOVE BOOK®
Jove Books are published by The Berkley Publishing Group,
a member of Penguin Putnam Inc.,
200 Madison Avenue, New York, New York 10016.
JOVE and the "J" design are trademarks belonging to
Jove Publications, Inc.

PRINTED IN THE UNITED STATES OF AMERICA

10 9 8 7 6 5 4 3 2 1

For Lee Goggins, who gave me shelter at High Lonesome
during the Republic of Texas Insurrection
May 5, 1997

SLOCUM AND THE
GREAT DIAMOND HOAX

1

The roar of the water blasting against the side of the hill deafened John Slocum. He had to watch the mine foreman's face carefully not to miss a word of what the man was saying.

Lou Morgan shouted, "You have the look of a man who can use that. Can you?" Morgan pointed to the ebony-handled Colt Navy slung comfortably in Slocum's cross-draw holster. The foreman didn't seem upset at the notion he might be hiring a gunfighter. Not at all.

"Been known to use it if the need arose," Slocum said carefully. Spray from the high-pressure monitors filled the air and ran down his face like torrents of cold sweat. He turned to the gorge, where the streaming water gnawed away tons of dirt every hour, sending it all into a dirty river at the bottom of the gorge where it was carried away to ceaselessly rocking sluices. Tons of dirt clawed from the gorge produced pounds of gold every day. A man working by stint of backbreaking personal digging might get an ounce, if the strike was rich. The Gold Trident mine was poor, from all Slocum had heard, and yet the hydro-mine brought forth as much as two pounds of gold a day.

The ugly, raw slash in the land was offset by the dancing

1

rainbows in the misty air above. The pot of gold at the end of the rainbow, Slocum thought.

When the monitors were turned off and the ravening water vanished from the air, taking with it the lovely rainbow colors, only the grotesque two-hundred-foot-deep gorge would remain as mute testimony to the stark efficiency of hydraulic mining technology.

"We got an investment to protect," Morgan shouted. "Come on into the shack. Not much quieter, but we can still talk better." Slogging through the ankle-deep mud, the foreman went to the small shack built against an outcropping of rock not as easily blown apart by even the powerful water jetting from the monitors. Morgan slammed the door shut behind him.

They still had to shout to be heard.

"I need protection, Slocum. I'm willing to pay top dollar to keep trespassers off the land."

"Why bother?" Slocum asked. "Nobody without one of those monitors and all the pumps that feed it is going to sneak in and high-grade you."

"I didn't say thieves. The company's got guards for our shipments into San Francisco."

"You don't keep the gold in Oroville?" Slocum had not ridden through the small town that owed its existence to this mine. Instead, he had come in from the east, straight from Virginia City over in Nevada. The taste of gold and silver there had sparked his interest in the job he had heard about from a man heading in the opposite direction.

"No vault strong enough. Safer to ship to the banks in San Francisco," Morgan said. "But that's no concern of yours. Mr. Emerson wants to keep prowlers off our land."

"Emerson? The Gold Trident's owner?"

"None other than," Morgan said proudly, as if Slocum must have heard of the man's fame and riches. Slocum hadn't. "We been having trouble with them rabble-rousing groups over in Oroville. Just keep 'em off our property and I'll pay you fifteen dollars a week, plus a bunk and grub with the mining crew.''

"You run the mine twenty-four hours a day?''

"Mr. Emerson wants us to, but there's always problems doing it at night. A pump busts and how do you fix it? By feel? And aiming gets to be a chore too. No sense missing promising deposits. Nope, sunup to sundown. It's the sundown-to-sunup shift you'd be working to protect the mine.''

Slocum considered the offer. It was mighty generous. Sixty dollars a month was more than most sheriffs earned. And they didn't get a bunk. What they did get was peace and quiet. There'd be no way Slocum could sleep with the constant roar of the high-pressure water cannon ripping out the earth's guts. Still, it wouldn't be hard to ride a few miles away and find a peaceful spot to sleep in the woods. His bedroll could be mighty comfortable if he made a mattress of pine needles and got all the rocks out from under him.

"Who's likely to come up here?''

"People intent on destroyin' what they can't get for themselves.''

"Miners you fired?''

"Why does it matter?'' Morgan asked sharply.

"Figure some kid looking to toss stones into the gorge is a mite different from a man all likkered up and looking to get even for being fired.''

"Won't be either of them,'' Morgan said, his lips curling in irritation at being interrogated. "You in or you out?''

"In,'' Slocum decided. He shook the foreman's hand, wondering what he had gotten himself into. If it didn't work out to his liking, he could always move on at the end of a week fifteen dollars richer, which was more than he had in his jeans at the moment.

"Good. I knew you was the man for us. Why don't you wander around and get the lay of the land? Looks a mite different after dark. Wouldn't want you taking a wrong step. It's a long ways to the bottom." Lou Morgan chuckled and opened the door. New sounds assaulted Slocum's ears, taking the edge off his usually keen hearing.

He followed the foreman outside, wiped water from his eyes constantly, and wondered if he ought to wear his yellow slicker. It wouldn't take but a few minutes near a monitor to be soaked to the skin. Wet clothes didn't bother him as much as having his six-shooter seize up when he needed it most. The Colt Navy was like a fine watch. It required careful tending to remain reliable.

Slocum pulled down the brim of his dripping Stetson as he made his way to the edge of the gorge. A moment of vertigo caught him in its grip. He wobbled slightly, only to have a strong hand grab his arm and pull him back.

"Everybody gets that way at first. You learn," shouted a small man with sandy hair and hands twice what Slocum would have expected. "My name's Wyoming."

Slocum nodded and glanced over his shoulder into the deep trench. It seemed to go to the bottom of the world. The hard-blasting water from a half-dozen monitors along this side of the Gold Trident added water and dirt from the far bank at a prodigious rate. Staring down gave him vertigo, and watching the relentless slide of gold-filled dirt into the pit hypnotized him.

"It's the sound," Wyoming shouted. "It turns off most all the senses and makes it easy to simply float along as if you'd tied one on. Only, there's never a hangover." He laughed. "Morgan tole me to see you to a bunk and some grub. You don't have the look of a hydro-miner about you. Ever work hardrock?"

"Some," Slocum allowed. "Never liked being underground for so much of my life."

"Know what you mean. I threw in with some of them Cornish coal miners out Cripple Creek way a few years ago. Hated it. They loved it. They was right at home buried a mile underground. Even my Anne didn't like the place, so we moved on."

"Morgan hired me as a mine guard," Slocum said as they walked along. "Who's he talking about wanting to hurt this place?"

Wyoming scratched his head, shook dirt and water from his sandy hair, and pointed into the side of the hill. The miners used a petered-out mine shaft for their bunkhouse. Inside, the sound almost vanished, but the ground shook constantly, as if an earthquake rocked the land.

"We got some hotheads what don't see how good the mine is for Oroville, that's all. They make some trouble, they feel good about shoutin' and pissin' into the wind, and then go home. Mr. Emerson, he's been worrying more and more about this here mine."

"Why?" Slocum sat at a table and worried open a can of beans Wyoming set in front of him. A dirty spoon scooped out the beans just fine, and added some needed flavor as he wolfed down the tin-bitter contents.

"Production has been declinin' something fierce. Might be about at the end of the vein. Tore up an entire mountain in the year we been sprayin'," Wyoming said. "Couldn't expect the mine to last forever, not at the rate we eat dirt."

"So what does Emerson care then?" Slocum finished the beans and looked longingly at a can of peaches. Wyoming silently shoved it across the table to him. It had been too long between meals, and this filled the hollow spot in Slocum's belly.

"Matter of principle, maybe. I think it has to do with not wantin' to get pushed around. He's got another mine a hundred miles from here, on up north, and if protests over this one gather support, he might have to shut that one down too.''

"From what the foreman said, this mine is the reason Oroville even exists. Why would the townspeople want the mine closed?''

"Hotheads. Some of them suffragists. We got a bunch of them in Wyoming. They get frustrated and turn to bustin' up saloons or findin' other reasons to make mischief. Some even want to vote. This bunch says the mine is ruinin' the countryside's beauty, as if any of them so much as rode past in the past dozen years to look at it.''

"Are they likely to start shooting?''

"Shooting?'' Wyoming laughed. "Most of them are women. What men ride with them are preachers and the like. I reckon Morgan just wants you to shoo them away. Seeing a man with a piece like yours hangin' at his side might make 'em piss their pants, yes, sir.''

With that, Wyoming patted a bunk for Slocum to stow his gear in and left. Slocum finished the peaches, thinking on the real reason Morgan had hired him. If a bunch of womenfolk wanted to shout and wave signs, they'd get mighty wet and never be heard over the bedlam created by the straining steam-powered pumps and the water-belching monitors.

Slocum curled up on the hard bunk and was asleep within minutes, the constant shiver of the bed reminding him of sleeping on a train.

The shift coming in to hang their oilskins and get some food awoke him. Slocum stretched, jumped to the floor, and got some curious stares from the hydro-miners. Wyoming came in and introduced Slocum around. When he finished, the men were even more distant. Slocum realized they thought they were sleeping with a hired killer.

He had done more than his share of killing, but never for money. He always had good reasons when he pulled the trigger on a man. More often than not it was a matter of surviving, but Slocum wasn't above taking revenge if the circumstances warranted it. He had met men meaner than any stepped-on rattler. They deserved killing. It was a purging that saved more lives, maybe innocent lives, later on.

And sometimes Slocum had even felt good about it. He didn't figure this guard job would require any shooting. For all that, he was happy enough. Leaving Nevada had not been entirely up to him. The law might even have a wanted poster out for him, as if that concerned him overly. The minor charges would be long forgotten when the first wanted poster was still being tacked up on marshals' walls.

During the war, Slocum had ridden with Quantrill's Raiders, and had had a run-in with his commanding officer and Bloody Bill Anderson after the Lawrence, Kansas, raid. Slocum had had no problem shooting down Federals, especially if they were shooting at him, but Quantrill had carried warfare to unacceptable levels when he had ordered any male over the age of eight slaughtered on sight. Slocum had been sure younger children had been cut down by the bloodthirsty guerrillas riding into town that day.

For his complaints, Slocum had been gutshot and left for dead. Too ornery to die, he had recovered slowly and returned to the family farm in Calhoun, Georgia, only to find his parents dead. Slocum had worked the farm, in the family since King George II had deeded it to his ancestors, and regained his full strength. The carpetbagger judge sent in after the war to oversee Reconstruction had taken a fancy to the land, thinking on it for a stud farm.

No taxes had been paid, the judge had said. He and a hired gunman had ridden out in the warm morning Georgia sun to seize Slocum's Stand. That afternoon, Slocum had mounted and ridden West, leaving behind two fresh graves under the afternoon shadow cast by the springhouse. Dogging his steps ever since had been the wanted posters. No one forgave judge-killing, even when it was a needed and necessary chore.

Slocum glanced at his yellow slicker, then decided he didn't need it now that the monitors had been turned off. He settled the gun at his left hip, noticed the uneasiness of the miners, then stepped into the biting night air, still damp from the millions of gallons of water pumped against the far bank of the gorge.

"Ready to start patrol, Slocum?" came Lou Morgan's loud voice. Slocum turned, wondering why the man was still shouting. Then it occurred to him that the foreman's hearing might be gone from the constant blare during the day.

"Getting around to seeing where there might be any trouble," Slocum agreed.

"Heard tell from some of the men there might be a passel of them rabble-rousers coming out here tonight. You keep 'em at bay, you hear? I don't want any trouble. Mr. Emerson's going to be in town sometime soon."

"We wouldn't want any trouble for Mr. Emerson," Slocum said dryly. The sarcasm passed Lou Morgan by. The foreman went off, muttering to himself. Slocum continued his slow circuit of the perimeter of the hydraulic mining camp. He found a vantage point high above where the steep drop had been cut away using the force of the water. From there, he could sit and take in the road to Oroville and the camp and the heavy pumps and monitors that spewed out the water. If any trouble developed, he might have a quick run getting back, but he ought to have plenty of warning from there.

He'd only settled down when he saw torches bouncing along the road from town. Heaving to his feet, Slocum got back to the gate on the road as several dozen men and women waving signs and stabbing at the air with their sputtering pitch torches reached the Gold Trident signpost.

"Evening," Slocum said loudly enough to get their attention. "What can I do for you folks?"

"Close down the mine! It's raping the land!" shouted one man. Slocum turned his gaze toward the man. He shrank back, clutching his sign like a drowning man might hold onto a rescue rope.

"Don't think that's anything I can do," Slocum said.

"What you *can* do is stand aside," a woman with fiery red hair said angrily. "We intend to burn this place to the ground! What ground that's been left!"

Slocum studied the woman. Her skin was milky white and smoother than silk. Her wild red hair was in disarray, but it circled her oval face like a delicate picture frame. She was tall, maybe five feet nine, but the difference in height between her and the six-foot Slocum made no difference. She moved forward, her chin thrust out defiantly. From this position, Slocum couldn't help noticing she certainly filled the gingham dress she wore. She stopped short of banging up against him as she shouted her slogans.

"Don't mean much since you're not getting in," Slocum said. "You got a grievance, take it to Mr. Emerson, the owner. He's supposed to be in town soon."

The woman looked startled at this. She quickly recovered. This time she did bang up against Slocum. He found it more delightful than threatening.

"You let us by, hear? We won't stand for the natural beauty of the land being destroyed like this. Henry David Thoreau said—"

"What do you hear from Walden Pond?" asked Slocum. Again he'd stopped her diatribe. She had no answer. "Reckon even Mr. Thoreau might find it a bit extreme of you trying to burn down buildings and kill people."

"We will be as violent as necessary to stop this atrocity!"

"Not tonight. Do it all legal, and I'll step aside. Get a judge to order the mine shut down."

A ripple of whispers passed through the crowd. By not meeting their threats with force, Slocum had taken the wind from their sails. Some backed down, but not the woman. The redhead stood her ground.

"We will not cotton to more destruction of our lovely countryside!"

"Then do something that will stop it. This won't. You're not getting past me." Slocum stepped back and simply stood, relaxed—as relaxed as a mountain lion ready to pounce. The men backed off even more, taking the other women with them. Even the firebrand leading them realized she had met her match.

"You mark my words, this isn't the last you'll hear of us." With that she turned and flounced off. Slocum admired the way her bustle rolled from side to side. Then the darkness swallowed her and her throng, even their torches vanishing in the inky black of a moonless night within a minute.

Slocum let out a sigh. He wished all his jobs were this easy. Turning, he almost ran into Lou Morgan.

"That—that Carrie Sinclair!" sputtered the foreman. "Next time you see that bitch, I want you to put a bullet in her, Slocum."

"She seemed reasonable enough, if you mean the red-haired woman," Slocum said.

"She's a devil. She's crazy. She's responsible for trying to get the Gold Trident closed. I don't want you mollycoddling her. You see her here again, you ventilate her. That's an order!" Morgan stormed off, grumbling to himself. Slocum wondered how much of the confrontation the foreman had overheard. Most, he supposed. This told Slocum Lou Morgan was the kind of man who let others fight his battles.

That didn't bother him overmuch. It simply defined the

man who had hired him. Slocum made a slow circuit of the area, then had started back to his lookout point when he heard someone stub a toe and curse under his breath. Frowning, Slocum homed in on the sound and advanced cautiously. Although he didn't think so, someone from the mob might have sneaked around intent on mischief.

Ahead stood the large pumps that forced huge torrents of water through the monitors. Slocum looked around, trying to figure if Morgan might have come this way. From the direction he'd headed, the foreman had probably gone back to the bunkhouse buried in the side of the hill. Someone else was out there. Slocum heard another curse, then caught the flare of a lucifer.

And a glint of steel. The man with the match also carried a knife.

"Hoses," Slocum said to himself, seeing the thick fabric-wrapped pipes that fed water from the pumps into the nozzles. He had seldom seen any this large. They had to be specially fabricated—and that made them expensive. Expensive and probably damned hard to replace should anything happen to them.

Walking faster, Slocum skirted the head-high pumps and worked forward, toward the monitors secured on the hillside. He wished there had been more light, but knew the darkness hid his advance from the unseen man even as it hid the man working hard on the hose.

"Move and I'll drill you," Slocum called, wondering what reaction he would get. He was not expecting the gunshot that tore through the air to the left of his ear. Ducking instinctively saved him from the second slug that would have blown off his head.

He hit the ground, grunted, and got his six-gun out. Rather than firing blindly, he waited for a decent target. A foot-long tongue of flame licked in his direction as the unseen man fired. Slocum lined up his barrel and fired. He was rewarded with a yelp, but he knew the bullet had only winged the other gunman. From the sucking sound of boots in the thick mud, Slocum knew the other man was high-tailing it.

Dashing around the jungle of pumps and hoses, Slocum got a brief look at the man's silhouette as he ran away, downhill toward the mouth of the gold mine gorge. Slocum fired twice more, missing both times. But he slowed the other's escape enough to close the distance between them.

Slocum didn't bother yelling out threats or entreaties to surrender. It would be a waste of time. If the man was willing to kill the instant he was discovered, he had been up to something that was both illegal and dangerous. Slocum fired another round, but it went wide. He considered reloading before plunging on into the darkness after his assailant, then hesitated. He had not brought along a spare cylinder, believing the guard duty would be peaceable.

The unfamiliar ground proved treacherous for him. He slipped and slid a dozen feet down the incline before fetching up against a stump. Slocum moaned, hoping he hadn't broken a rib. Carefully coming to his knees, Slocum listened hard and waited for movement. He had to make every shot count.

Movement. He got to his feet and advanced in a crouch, ready to fire when he got a clear target. Slocum moved closer to the edge of the gorge slashed in the land by the hydraulic water cannon. The drop here wasn't as bad as up at the top. Slocum couldn't make out the bottom, but it wasn't more than twenty feet, not the two hundred where the monitors worked.

Walking parallel to the cut, he made his way downhill. The trees in the gorge had had their roots cut from under them and had slid down into the gorge in a slow pantomime of death. Slocum wondered how the crew at the bottom working the sluice tables got rid of entire pine trees. Then he found more to occupy him than idle speculation about mine operation.

Darkness moved across darkness ahead. He lifted his six-shooter and took careful aim at the space between two rough-barked trees on the edge of the gorge. Their limbs framed a perfect shot. During the war Slocum had been a sniper and a good one, sitting on a hill most of the day waiting for the one shot that would turn a battle. Without an officer, the Federals often fell apart in battle. He would spot a glint of sunlight off gold braid, squeeze gently, feel the Brown Bess kick, and the tide of battle would be turned.

He showed the same patience now. A snap of a twig, a slight movement, and he lifted his pistol and readied himself for the shot.

His eyes widened when he saw the faint outline of a deer and knew he had the wrong target. As this revelation hit him, so did a long branch from an oak tree. The heavy limb smashed into the side of his head, sending him flying into the air—and to the bottom of the gorge, where the rushing torrents still brought down sludge from higher in the hydraulic mine.

2

He fell endlessly, head spinning faster than his body. Then Slocum hit the muddy water with a *splash*!

Gasping, sputtering, he was sucked under the racing water. Only his instinct for survival kept him thrashing about until he found a log the size of a battering ram to grab onto. Blind from the silt, buffeted by the rushing water, mouth full of foul debris, Slocum did nothing but let the swift current drag him and his lifesaving raft down the stream. Slocum spat hard and got some of the mud cleared from his windpipe, and only then did he struggle to get atop the slowly rotating log.

He slipped, and was almost tossed into the river to fend for himself. He clung to the log as if he was breaking the orneriest starfishing stallion that ever pranced on the earth. Slocum's strong legs held him firmly in place, and his balance kept him on top. For the moment.

He wiped the water from his eyes and cursed when he saw the sluice tables ahead. It wasn't much of a fall into the equipment, but it would be his end if he went through the screened sluices in his current battered condition. Swinging around, he got his boots pressed on the rough side of the log, then launched himself for the distant shoreline. It proved a harder swim than he anticipated, but he succeeded in dragging himself onto the low bank. Shaking like a wet dog, Slocum sent water droplets flying in all directions.

Then he sat and swore at his ambusher. Slocum's hand went to his holster. The ebony-handled .31-caliber Colt Navy was lost in the river. He had its twin in his bedroll, but the loss infuriated him more than the near-brush with death. A panicky hand flew to his watch pocket in his vest.

"Still there," he sighed. His only legacy from his brother Robert, killed at Gettysburg in Pickett's insane charge, had not been dislodged. He dried off the case, popped it open, and was pleased to see it still gave the proper time.

Slocum frowned. It was running. It couldn't lie to him. How the entire fight had lasted less than five minutes was beyond him. Slocum felt as if he had been shooting and drowning for hours.

"Don't know who you are, but you're mine," Slocum promised as he stood and got his bearings. His angry eyes scanned the high edges of the gorge for any trace of his assailant. Nothing moved up there that wasn't part of the landscape. A few trees shifted and swayed in a gentle breeze. But no human peered over to see if the fall had killed John Slocum.

z   Getting to the top of the gorge where the monitors stood like silent sentinels proved the work of an hour. The steep banks afforded no handholds, forcing him to circle and come up to the camp on the main road. The bunkhouse was silent. Slocum considered fetching his backup six-shooter, then decided against it. He'd have to explain how he ended up looking like a drowned rat.

He could stand the jeers and taunts of the miners over the fall. He wasn't up to confessing he had also lost his six-gun.

Like a soggy ghost, he drifted among the monitors and

found where the intruder had sawed and hacked at a high-pressure hose. If the miners turned on the pumps with the hose half cut the way it was, the blowout might send the line snapping about like a boiling mad rattler. Some of the crew might be killed. Worse, Slocum suspected, the foreman would not want to see valuable equipment out of business for even a few minutes.

From all Slocum saw and heard, this mine had run its race. Trying to leach out the last flake of gold seemed useless to him, but Slocum wasn't getting paid to tell Emerson what to do with his property.

He found the tracks left by the intruder and followed them carefully. Whoever it had been, it was a man. Slocum remembered what Lou Morgan had said about the woman from town. Carrie Sinclair had not left these prints, not unless she wore a boot bigger than Slocum's and outweighed him by at least twenty pounds.

Occasionally dropping to his belly to peer closely at the prints, Slocum found where he had been attacked. He saw how the man had simply stood in shadows and waited.

"He's got guts, I'll give him that," Slocum said. It took iron nerve to simply abide until the proper instant. Going to his belly again, Slocum moved around like a human snake. He grinned broadly at his good fortune when he saw something hard and dark sticking up out of the mud. He grabbed and tugged his Colt Navy from the muck.

Slocum sat and worried out mud from the barrel and cylinder, seeing it wouldn't be reliable until he had properly cleaned it. But it felt good weighing down his left hip again. With the satisfying presence of the six-shooter in his holster, he continued his hunt. From the edge of the gorge the tracks led into a stand of trees a dozen yards from the verge. The powerful water monitors had yet to turn on the ground under the trees, but they already leaned as if their roots were being sucked into the pit caused by the hydro-mining.

In the pine-needle-strewn area Slocum came to the end of the tracks. He worked for over an hour trying to find where the man had run. He had two possible trails, but they looked old to him, days old. In resignation, he hiked back up the slope toward the main camp. Settling down with an old rag he found, he set to work cleaning his six-shooter. The chore was done before sunup.

A few of the miners came from their bunkhouse, stretching and yawning. They laughed and nudged each other when they saw Slocum's condition. Wyoming finally came out, gnawing on a hard hunk of bread. He grinned broadly and slapped Slocum on the shoulder.

"Fell into the gorge, did you now?"

"Something like that," Slocum admitted.

"It happens to everyone. Last night there wasn't much of a moon. Made it easier to lose your way, betcha. Just stand around the monitors for a spell, and you'll get yourself hosed down." Wyoming's eyes dropped to the clean six-shooter. He started to comment, then bit back his question. Shaking his head, he joined the others preparing the water cannon for another day of ripping away the earth.

"Wyoming!" Slocum called.

"Yeah?"

"Check all the hoses before you put pressure on them. Especially the hose on that monitor." Slocum pointed to the one the unknown man had been so intent on putting out of commission. Seeing Wyoming hesitate, Slocum added, "It'll only take you a minute, and Morgan will think you're a hero."

Wyoming frowned and shouted to the other miners in his crew. They set to work on their hoses. Excited shouts showed they had found the damage. Slocum went into the bunkhouse, eyed the hard bed, and knew he ought to get some sleep. He changed his clothes, bundled the dirty ones, then headed for Oroville. After last night, he had questions he wanted answered.

The ride into town seemed to take forever. When Slocum finally rounded a bend in the road, the pleasant little town spread out in front of him, much smaller now than it had been at some earlier time. He saw sections of town where the houses and stores were abandoned. The owners had simply walked away, leaving only the main street and a few lesser ones as the center of commerce.

Oroville was dying because the mine was dying, Slocum figured.

If the mine was destined to run down like a cheap watch sometime soon, why would anyone try to destroy the mining equipment?

"Someone who doesn't know the mine is on its last legs," Slocum mumbled to himself. "Someone who is intent on closing it down to keep the dirt in its original God-given place." Only one person he knew of in Oroville fit that description. If Carrie Sinclair had not hit him the night before, someone working with her probably had.

He dismounted in front of a barbershop. He had a job now and could afford the fifty cents for a hot bath and a shave.

"Howdy," the barber said, frowning when Slocum came in. "You passin' through?"

"Work at the mine," Slocum said. If the barber's attitude had been inhospitable before, it turned downright hostile now. Slocum wasn't sure he wanted a man with a straight razor and a bad demeanor near his throat.

Slocum paused, eyeing the man. The hot gaze faded a mite, but the barber remained contrary.

"You have something against miners?" Slocum asked.

"Trouble, you people are nothing but trouble."

"Seems Oroville is drying up and blowing away. Has the mine been cutting back lately?"

"Don't see hardly anybody from the mine in town anymore," the barber allowed.

"Then you won't mind taking my money." Slocum settled in the chair, wondering if he ought to keep his six-shooter in his hand as the man worked on the tough beard.

For a few minutes the barber worked in silence. Slocum relaxed and let the man drag the razor over neck and cheek. Actually performing his chosen profession loosened up the barber too.

"Nothing personal, you know," the barber said at length. "That fellow who owns the mine, Henry Emerson is his name, has not been too good for the town. Tried to rook us at every turn. And the gold from the mine doesn't even stay in town."

"Goes into San Francisco, from what I'm told," Slocum said.

"Right. We could sure use some wealth in our lone bank, greedy as its president is. If the mine closes down, the whole town might disappear."

"I'm confused. You like the mine there or not? I heard tell Carrie Sinclair is out to close it down. You for that?"

"Oh, her?" scoffed the barber. "She's a pretty one, she is, but a hothead. She blowed into town a while back, and it's been nothing but trouble swirling about her trim ankles."

"So you don't support her and the others wanting to shut down the mine?"

"I got feelings on both sides," the barber said. "The mine puffed up Oroville to three times its size before they started their demon's water hose. Everything was prosperous, or so it seemed. Now it's like they're sucking the blood from a dying carcass."

Slocum let the man continue the shave in silence. He thought hard. He understood the barber's contradictory attitudes. The mine brought in a rush of wealth, but at a huge cost. Now that the wealth was going away, receding like the ocean tide, any hope for real riches was going away too.

A promise no one in Oroville had wanted had been made—and now it was being broken and everyone in the town complained.

"What do you mean Miss Sinclair came to town a few weeks ago?" Slocum asked suddenly. "I thought she was a longtime resident."

"Her? No, sir. Nobody knows much about her. Came in on the stagecoach from San Francisco with a single trunk. Rented a room in Ma Perkins' place at the edge of town, all properlike. Then she set about givin' speeches and gettin' people hot under the collar about the mine, like it was some religious mission for her."

Carrie Sinclair seemed more of a mystery by the minute. And all the more attractive because of it. All through his bath he thought of the redhead and grew more curious.

"Come to Oroville just to close down the mine?" Slocum wondered to himself. He sank down in the galvanized tub and let the warm sudsy water cover his head. Then he surfaced. This dunking proved far better than the one he had endured the night before.

Dressing, he paid the barber and left, stepping into a warm sunlit morning. Puffs of white clouds moved sluggishly through the azure sky, threatening a rainstorm in the afternoon. Now, the day was about perfect. Slocum went hunting for Carrie Sinclair. With a few answers, the day *would* be perfect.

Finding the woman proved well nigh impossible. The townspeople wouldn't answer his questions and seemed to stare right through him, as if the bath had turned him clear as glass. Disgusted, he went into a saloon to get a beer and some food. Settling into a chair, he called to the barkeep, "Beer. And bring me a bowl of those pigs knuckles."

"Coming right up," the bartender said. The young man sported a big bushy mustache. As he turned, Slocum saw it partially hid a large scar on his left cheek that ran toward his lip.

"I'm so hungry I could eat everything including the pig's oink," Slocum said.

"I'll fix you up a sandwich then," the barkeep said. "You're about the only business I'll have until this evening. Maybe not much even then."

"I suppose it gets a bit rowdy after the shift at the mine," Slocum said.

"Not as many of them working up there now," the barkeep said, putting down a thick ham sandwich and beer. "Emerson is working them overtime 'cuz there's fewer of them. They're all tuckered out and only come to town now and again."

"That because of Carrie Sinclair?" Slocum asked, trying to sound disinterested. He saw the barkeep stiffen at the mention of the woman's name.

"We'd do about anything to keep the mine running," the barkeep said. "Who cares what it does to the ground up there? Worthless land, except for the gold buried there. Those miners were paid top dollar and spent like there was no tomorrow. Not now. Half the number at the mine as when they started. Fewer."

"You blame her? Miss Sinclair?"

"The bitch," growled the barkeep. "She didn't cause the problem, but she's not doing anything to help. With all the rabble-rousing she's doing, it's a civic duty Mr. Emerson is doing to keep that mine open. It is."

"Where can I find her? Might have a word or two with her about what she's doing."

The barkeep backed away from Slocum and stared at him, as if studying him closely for the first time.

"What's your interest?"

"I just got hired up at the Gold Trident. Guard," he said. "Lou Morgan suggested I might talk to Miss Sinclair and find out if there's any way to talk her out of her crusade."

"Lou said that?" The bartender laughed harshly. "More likely, he told you to put a bullet through her empty head." The barkeep blanched, swallowed hard, and backed off some more when he finally decided Slocum had the look of a killer about him. "Look, mister, I don't want any part of murdering a woman, even that hellion."

"Words, not bullets, that's what I want to toss around right now," Slocum said, finishing his sandwich and beer.

"She usually sets up a box at the end of town on the road leading to the mine. Anytime now. She harangues whoever'll stop and listen. Too danged many do, if you ask me. Anything that'll keep the mine open and the money flowing, I'm for it. Except murder," he added hastily.

"I'll let Hank Emerson know that," Slocum said wryly. He paid and left. He had wasted most of the day hunting for the elusive will-o'-the-wisp that was Carrie Sinclair. He had to report to the mine for another night of patrolling and preventing intruders from destroying the mining equipment.

Slocum worried he might not have time to find the red-haired woman and talk with her, but he quickly found her on a box, extolling the horrors of hydraulic mining. The setting sunlight caught her from behind, turning her hair into a golden crown. She cleared her throat and called out, "The mine is ruining this town. It is ruining our land. If you let them continue with their terrible water cannon, they will cut this whole world right in half!"

Looking around, Slocum saw that few bothered to gather and listen. This didn't stop Carrie Sinclair from her diatribe against the Gold Trident and its owner. He moved closer. She glared at him, but gave no other sign he even existed. After a few minutes of ranting without an audience, she calmed down.

"I have a question," Slocum said in a civil tone.

"What do you care about answers? You think you have them all!"

"Someone cut the hoses at the mine last night. You know anything about it?"

"I wish I'd done it, but I didn't," she said.

"I know it wasn't you. Not personally," Slocum said. "I'm thinking it might be one of those fine citizens who came with you to the mine last night."

"If you think a crime has been committed, see the marshal. I am not going to testify against anyone doing the right thing. I'm only sorry more damage wasn't done."

"So you know how much was done?" asked Slocum, a harder edge coming to his voice. "The man with the knife tried to kill me. Damned near succeeded. I'm supposed to stop men like that from doing any damage, but he turned it personal when he ambushed me."

"What?" Her eyes widened. He saw she had marvelous green eyes, with a tiny dark spot near her left pupil. Somehow, this slight imperfection made her all the lovelier.

"Destroy equipment, I lose my job. Bushwhack me and it gets personal."

"The marshal, he—"

"This is between me and a mangy coyote who's more than willing to kill from hiding."

"I don't want anyone hurt," she said. "I don't think any of my followers would resort to such violence, but—"

"But you aren't sure?"

"I'm sorry, Mr.—"

"Slocum. John Slocum."

"Carrie Sinclair," she said, impulsively thrusting out her hand. Slocum wasn't sure if she expected him to kiss it or shake it. The need to decide which evaporated when angry shouts came from down the street. A dozen miners were shaking their fists and shouting threats. The best Slocum could tell, they were all in a lather over something Carrie had done or said, and they intended to have it out with her.

"You don't look too popular at the moment. Why don't you find somewhere to ride out the storm?"

"I will *not*," she said, stamping her foot. Slocum noticed two things. It was sizes smaller than the boot prints he had followed. And the barber was right. Carrie Sinclair had quite a nicely turned ankle.

The crowd got closer, and Slocum instinctively put himself between them and the woman. Carrie pushed around him to face the miners directly.

"Have you all finally come to your senses? Are you quitting the mine to—" She never got any farther. Someone toward the back of the crowd threw a dirt clod at her. She ducked, but some flaked off and left a dirty streak in her red hair.

"You worthless bitch! They're firin' us because of you! Emerson is cuttin' back by half! Because you're stirrin' up so much trouble over in Sacramento!"

"What's happened?" Slocum asked the miner.

"Over in the capital. They're talkin' on outlawin' hydraulic mining altogether! Emerson says he has to let us go 'cuz of that. He might be closin' down the whole damned mine because of her!"

Slocum shoved the miner back when the man grabbed for Carrie.

"She's just one person," Slocum said. "Seems to me it takes more than a red-haired hellion to get a law passed banning hydraulic mining."

"She caused it. She cost me my job. She cost us all our jobs!"

Slocum glanced over his shoulder and saw Carrie was getting scared. That didn't surprise him. He wasn't too comfortable about the crowd either. Men who had lost their jobs too often thought they had nothing more to lose.

"You're working for the mine, Slocum," shouted one. "Get out of the way and let justice be done!"

"Justice is one thing, this is a lynching," Slocum said. "Miss Sinclair didn't commit any crime other than pissing you all off."

"Whose side are you on? Hers or ours?"

Slocum looked from the woman to the crowd and made his decision. He shoved back from the miner butting up against him, reached over, and took the leather thong off the hammer of his Colt Navy.

He squared his stance and stared straight at the man he thought was leader of the crowd.

"How loud do you want my answer to be?" he asked in a level voice that carried more menace than if he had shouted.

Slocum's fingers curled, and he settled his shoulders, getting ready to throw down on the miners.

3

Slocum's steely eyes fixed on the miner he took to be the leader. The man looked around nervously, licked his lips, and turned to see if he had any support from the others in the crowd. The miners recognized Slocum as the man Lou Morgan had hired to guard their mine at night, but they also saw death in a gunman's eyes. That was enough to make the unarmed men fade away. That left the solitary miner to face Slocum's wrath.

"You can't shoot me down. I ain't got a gun," the miner said. Seeing he was still alive after this utterance emboldened him. He thrust out his chin and called, "Let's settle this like men. Bare knuckles! Or do you have to hide behind that fancy six-shooter of yours?"

"Hold this," Slocum said, pulling out his Colt Navy and handing it to Carrie Sinclair. She took it with some authority, as if she would use it on the miner. Or maybe on Slocum. The look on her face told him she didn't know which side of the fence to come down on.

Slocum stepped up, judged his distance, and let fly. His fist connected with the tip of the miner's jaw, a hammer crashing into stone. Slocum winced as the shock went all the way into his shoulder. His hand hurt like hell, and he might have broken a knuckle in the punch. But the fight was over with that single punch.

The miner took a half step back. His eyes rolled up into his head, and he slumped to the ground as if some puppeteer had cut his strings. Slocum looked up and saw the rest of the miners muttering among themselves.

"I'm sorry you gents lost your jobs," Slocum said. "I work at the mine too, and reckon my job's not got long to run. But you don't take your wrath out on a lady, even one that might make you powerful angry."

The miners—the former miners—began edging away. Slocum's sharp command froze them in their tracks.

"Don't forget to take *him*. Here," he said, flipping a silver dollar onto the man's heaving chest. "Buy him a drink, if his jaw's not broken."

A pair of the men moved in and dragged off their friend. Slocum didn't see what happened to the silver cartwheel. It vanished and wasn't in the dust, so he reckoned someone who could use it had snared it. Only when it was apparent the danger was over did he turn back to Carrie.

"I'll take my six-gun now, ma'am," he said.

"Why'd you do that?" the redhead asked curiously. She made no move to return Slocum's gun.

"I don't think it's proper for a crowd to be threatening a lovely lady, no matter how much she tries to make them mad." He reached out and snared the Colt. A quick move had it back in the cross-draw holster.

"I'm not inciting them," Carrie said hotly. Her eyes flashed, and she looked all the prettier for the inner fire. "I have a mission. I do! Laugh if you like, but I will not see this beautiful land destroyed by hydraulic mining."

"Everyone's got to have a purpose. Good day." Slocum touched the brim of his Stetson and started off. She followed, matching his long stride.

"What's *your* purpose?" she asked.

"To see what's on the other side of the mountain. Not to get myself killed doing it."

"That's all?" she asked incredulously. "All you want to do is float along like some thistle on the wind and not get shot? What of the beauty around you?"

"You're about the most beautiful thing around me, and I don't see you're in any danger now. Excuse me. I have to get to work."

Slocum left the open-mouthed woman behind as he returned to the saloon to get his horse. He considered what he ought to do. If Morgan had laid off half the miners, for whatever reason, that didn't bode well for his own longevity on the job. The mine needed experienced miners a danged site more than it needed a guard who let himself get ambushed and dumped into the river at the bottom of the gorge.

He had yet to collect a paycheck at the mine. But if he simply rode away, he wouldn't be any worse off than he'd been the day before.

Except for one thing. He wanted to know who had almost killed him the night before. Until he settled that score, Slocum wasn't going to budge. With only slight reluctance Slocum returned to the mine for his shift of patrolling. Lou Morgan was a terror, roaring and shouting louder than the monitors still sending their prodigious torrents of water against the far bank of the gorge.

"Get out there right now, Slocum," the foreman shouted over the din. "It's gettin' near sundown, and I don't want none of the miners I just fired gettin' back at me."

"How many are left?" Slocum asked, looking around. He shook his head when he saw Wyoming and his crew making their way into the bunkhouse. They looked as if they had worked a hundred hours straight and then been beaten with whips for their effort.

"Half, less," Morgan said sullenly. "I don't want this

gettin' around, but you ought to know since you got to guard the equipment. We might be shuttin' the whole she-bang down soon.''

Slocum nodded. ''Anything to do with that woman from Oroville?''

''Sinclair?'' Morgan sneered. ''Her kind could never shut down the Gold Trident. No, this has to do with politics and what's goin' on over in San Francisco. And up in Sacramento.'' Morgan spat when he mentioned the name of the capital. ''They got their heads stuck up their asses, if you ask me, but no one ever does.''

With that the foreman stalked off. Slocum made his way to the bunkhouse and sat beside Wyoming. The man hardly acknowledged his presence.

''How long you figure we got before they get rid of the rest of us?'' asked Slocum.

''Not long. Shorty, Texas Jim, and some of the others they fired today were better at this style of mining than I am. Reckon it's time to think about moving on. Hate to do it too. The wife and family get their roots pulled up way too often.''

With that Wyoming turned and began eating listlessly, hardly tasting the foul vittles put out for the crew. Slocum noted other changes too. The men were not joking, and the pieces of equipment stored around the bunkhouse were gone. Outside, he'd seen wagons loading and lugging off spare equipment. What remained was being used, but nothing stayed in reserve. Even the reels of hose Wyoming had replaced were gone. The hose fed the powerful water cannon. If any more damage was done, that would shut down the mine.

Slocum didn't have to be a mining engineer to know what was happening. In a week, this mine would be closed down and Carrie Sinclair would be celebrating with her friends in Oroville.

He prowled the camp endlessly all night long, and saw nothing but a few coyotes coming in to sample the garbage left by the cook. Standing on the bank and staring into the racing current below, Slocum thought he detected a slackening of its headlong rush. Or maybe not. It could only have been his imagination.

But it had not been his imagination the night before when the man had tried to kill him. Slocum's hand rested on the ebony butt of his six-shooter as he thought on ways to track down that owlhoot and put an end to his backshooting ways.

Slocum slept until after noon, coming suddenly awake when he realized something was wrong. It took several seconds for him to realize what it was. Something was missing.

The deep gut-shaking vibration had stopped. He climbed from the bunk and hastily dressed, going out into the bright California sun. Squinting, he *heard* silence. Curious, he went over to the nearest monitor, where Wyoming and his crew just stood and stared at one another.

"Why'd you turn off that water cannon? The quiet's enough to spook a man," Slocum said.

"We're done," Wyoming said in dejection. "Finished. The mine's shut. Morgan got word from Mr. Emerson. We can pick up our pay at Morgan's cabin, but that's it. No more mining." Wyoming stared out into the distance, as if he saw something more than an empty hole.

Slocum realized he did. Wyoming and the others saw their livelihood disappearing. He hadn't heard of any other hydraulic mines in the vicinity, except the one Emerson ran a hundred miles away. And the politicians were working hard to outlaw the practice. In a way, Slocum thought it was for the best. Neither man nor land tolerated the roar and gouging wet knife of a monitor, not for long. A man might last a while longer, but eventually the vibration and noise would ruin him.

Step into the front of a monitor just being turned on, and it was worse than walking in front of a real cannon firing.

"Where you going to go?" Slocum asked.

"Can't say. Might head back to the Comstock. Or up north. Heard tell there's a big strike in Alaska. Hate the weather and I don't know anything about the Yukon, but I can learn. Have to leave the family behind, but if the pay's good, I can send them enough every month to live." Wyoming turned desolate eyes on Slocum. "Fact is, Slocum, I just don't know."

Slocum made his way to the bunkhouse, gathered his gear, and went to Morgan's office. Only a handful of miners were lined up to get their pay. He realized most of the rest had already been sent packing.

"Sorry you have to go after only two days," Morgan said, "but nobody's happy over it. Emerson said close it down, the mine's not valuable any more."

"What's its assay?"

"Three ounces a ton at its peak," Lou Morgan said. "The yield was dropping fast. The vein had petered out, and the sand didn't have enough dust in it to make the operation pay. Dammit." He shoved four dollars in rumpled greenbacks toward Slocum. "Thanks for all you done. Consider the extra a bonus."

"What extra?" Slocum said, stuffing the bills in his shirt pocket. He had earned every penny and maybe more. Without another word, he turned and left, got his horse, and rode back to Oroville. Without any clear direction to drift, he decided to spend a day or two in the town before making his decision.

He still had unfinished business with a no-account bushwhacker. If he hadn't flushed the varmint in two days, he'd let it go. The West was full of men he owed as much—or more—to. One more left to do his worst wouldn't cause Slocum to lose any sleep. Or not much.

Slocum hitched his horse outside a saloon and went inside. He saw a tight knot of miners. They glared at him. He thought he recognized one of the men from the run-in earlier, but he couldn't be sure. It didn't matter. Nothing mattered right now but putting some whiskey into his belly.

"A shot," he called to the barkeep. The man, about Slocum's age, waddled over and poured a stiff drink into a dirty glass. Slocum sucked in his breath, then knocked back the liquor. It was as potent as it looked.

"Nitric acid," the barkeep said in answer to the unspoken question. "Gives the kick of a mule in every shot."

"Again," Slocum said. He reached into his pocket to pull out one of the greenbacks he had received in pay at the mine, but a hand restrained him.

"No, my good man, no! I will buy you another shot of this magnificent distillate. Leave the bottle. Do and we shall all celebrate." The man doing the talking was a head shorter than Slocum, florid and almost cherubic. His round face beamed as he waved about a sheaf of greenbacks thick enough to choke a cow.

"Mister, I appreciate the offer of a free drink. Now if you'll take my advice, put away your money. Flashing it around like that will only lead to big trouble." Slocum inclined his head in the direction of the miners sitting at a table halfway across the saloon. They had lost their jobs, and now were being taunted by a fistful of scrip.

"Yes, yes, quite so, I see. My exuberance overwhelmed me. Leave the bottle, bartender. My friend and I will enjoy its full aromatic import."

"Don't know exactly what you said, but your money's good," the barkeep said, shoving the bottle across.

"My name is Astin Barclay. By profession I am, uh, well, let's say I find things."

"Are these things you find lost?" asked Slocum, sipping slowly at the potent liquor.

"Ah, a man of intelligence and discerning tastes." Barclay moved closer and whispered conspiratorially, "I find these. I am quite good at finding the blue clay where they reside too."

Slocum blinked at the rock Barclay dropped onto the bar. It had the look of something substantial, but he didn't know why.

"You are not a miner, are you?" Barclay asked under his breath. "Then you would not recognize what this is."

Slocum hefted the rock. It had aggregate hanging onto it, but the center was milky and had one sharp edge. He drew it across the shot glass. It left a deep cut.

"Ah, you are far more knowledgeable than most of these louts! I knew it the instant I saw you!"

"This is a diamond?" asked Slocum.

"It is, sir. I found it."

"And you want to sell it." Slocum felt a blanket of weariness descend on him. He had no time for con artists flashing fake stones. For all he knew, a hundred kinds of worthless stones would also score glass. He didn't intend to buy anything from Mr. Astin Barclay, even if he had the money.

"Yes, yes, but certainly not here, not to you. I am taking it into San Francisco where I can be paid well for it. And to conduct other business." Barclay turned shifty now, looking around.

"You found this near Oroville?"

"Sir, I would hire you as my confidential assistant, to guard my back and to be sure no brigands make off with this valuable stone."

"Put it in a bank," Slocum suggested.

"I must take it to San Francisco," Barclay insisted. "I can pay you well. What were you getting at the mine?"

Barclay stepped back a pace and studied Slocum carefully. "You were not grubbing in the muck, not you. I take you to be a foreman there. Or a shift leader or whatever they choose to name their most trusted men placed in positions of authority."

Slocum looked at Barclay as if he had crawled out from under a rock in the noonday sun.

"I was a guard," Slocum said.

"Better and better, my good man! I need protection, I do."

"You need a dose of horse sense," Slocum said. "You don't go flashing that wad of greenbacks around where anyone can see." His eyes drifted back to the rock on the bar. He wondered if it was real—and if Barclay had come by that roll of bills he showed around by selling another diamond. Curiosity was getting the better of Slocum. Besides, he had nowhere in particular to go. As he'd told Carrie Sinclair, he simply found a likely spot on the horizon and rode for it.

Getting paid for doing what he was intending to do seemed a decent thing to do. But something about Barclay put Slocum on edge, something more than the man's grandiose gestures. Slocum couldn't shake the feeling their paths had crossed, but he couldn't nail down when or where.

Barclay interrupted his thoughts. "You are just the man to provide me with, shall we say, frontier savvy? Is that the term?" He canted his head to one side, studying Slocum. Slocum suddenly felt like a bug under a magnifying glass. For all the man's pomposity, there was shrewdness lurking underneath.

"You could use that term," Slocum said dryly. "All you looking for is to be escorted to San Francisco? That's only a day's travel."

"Perhaps there would be more to the job, but only after

I get this appraised.'' Barclay reached over and laid his hand on the stone as if he stroked a lover's cheek. ''How about it, pahdner?''

''I'm not your partner, and I can ride along with you to San Francisco,'' Slocum said, wondering what he was getting himself into.

The smile on Astin Barclay's face was one of pure delight.

4

"Splendid, my good man, utterly splendid. You can, of course, start work for me at this very instant?" Astin Barclay gave Slocum that same look as before, as if pulling apart a bug and wondering what the detached legs were good for.

"Reckon so," Slocum said, pushing the potent liquor from him. His head spun a little. He had intended getting drunk, then finding a hotel room, figuring he would leave after two days if he couldn't track down the bushwhacker from the Gold Trident. Now he had an alternative. "Reckon I will, if the money is good."

"Sir, it shall be. And it will become even better!" Barclay moved closer to Slocum and whispered in a conspiratorial manner, looking around the saloon as if everyone wanted to crowd close and overhear what he had to say. "Will you come with me this moment on a small journey of exploration?"

"Where?" Slocum licked his lips, wondering if he ought to finish the whiskey before agreeing to anything. Or was it the whiskey that had made him agree to escort this popinjay to San Francisco? The rock Barclay stroked repeatedly might be worthless. Slocum didn't know, and he didn't

36

think any miner in Oroville would. They were gold miners. Maybe a few had worked silver mines or something else. Wyoming had mentioned working in Cripple Creek with Cornish coal miners. But diamonds? Slocum knew damned little about them, like everyone else within shouting distance.

"To the mine where they fired those hideous water cannon," Barclay said. "I must look for more. . . ." His voice trailed off as two miners blundered past, both drunker than lords.

"Don't know everyone's left the mine yet," Slocum said. "Why not wait a spell until we could poke around without someone like the foreman looking over our shoulders?"

"A capital idea! I am so glad I hired you on. Here, take this as a retainer." The stout man shoved across a hundred dollars from his bankroll. Slocum took the greenbacks quickly and thrust them into his shirt pocket. In a town where the main source of income had just vanished, it wasn't too smart letting anyone else see such wealth.

They were as like to kill him for the sheer sport of it—or out of frustration—as they were to ask for a loan to keep them going. Truth was, if Wyoming or some of the others Slocum had taken a shine to asked, he might have spotted them the money.

"Early," Barclay said, getting into the spirit of their venture. "Early tomorrow morning. After the sun has had a chance to stretch its fiery arms and embrace the world and we each have had a hearty breakfast. I shall meet you at the livery. Is this satisfactory?"

"I'll be there," Slocum said, reaching for the whiskey bottle. He watched Barclay leave, then eyed the level in the bottle. He sighed, and pushed away from him. He wanted a clear head. Somehow, he figured he would need it. He left the bottle where it was and walked to the crooked door leading into Oroville's main street. Behind him in the saloon he heard miners fighting over the abandoned bottle and its contents.

Slocum never looked back as he stepped into the heat of the day. He stood for a moment, letting the sun warm his face. Then he started walking, not sure where he headed. The activity let him think and look as if he had a purpose. The townsfolk seemed even more sullen than they had the day before when Slocum had asked around. He knew they had gazed into their own futures and seen nothing but darkness. With the hydraulic mine closed, they might as well close their businesses and ride on, hunting for more prosperous territory.

Hardly knowing it, Slocum found himself at the edge of town where Carrie Sinclair had stood on her box and harangued the crowd the prior afternoon. Her box still stood at the edge of the road, but of the flaming red-haired woman he saw no trace.

He tried to remember the name of the boardinghouse where she stayed, but couldn't. Slocum shrugged it off. He had no reason to hunt her down. Still, something about her intrigued him. He admired her fire and her devotion to a cause, even if it was one he thought bordered on the absurd.

"Mr. Slocum!" came the call from inside a nearby abandoned building. Slocum turned, hand moving in the direction of his six-shooter. He paused when he saw the woman standing silhouetted in the doorway. With the light behind her, he saw every womanly flare and curve on Carrie Sinclair's body. As she turned sideways and the light moved past her breasts and face and hair, he swallowed hard. She was one mighty fine-looking woman.

"You move like a striking snake," Carrie said, no sting in the words. If anything, she seemed to think this was a compliment. So did Slocum.

"Are you worried about my fangs?"

"Oh, no, sir, I am not," she said, stepping into the full daylight. "I saw you standing there and wondered if I might ask a favor."

"What might it be?" Slocum wasn't sure what she could want—or what he would agree to, simply to be with her a few more minutes.

"The mine has closed," she said, knowing full well everyone in town, including Slocum, had heard. "I would like to go out there to document what has been done to the ground. I want to give full testimony before the state legislature so no other hydraulic mine can destroy our lovely—"

"You want me to go with you?" Slocum asked, cutting off her diatribe against the mining companies. "Why me?"

"You are an honorable man," she said, her green eyes sparkling. She stepped closer. Slocum felt the heat from her body. Or was it only from the sun?

"You make hasty decisions," Slocum said.

"Hasty, perhaps, but they are usually right when it comes to people." She locked her arm in his and guided him back into the abandoned building. Slocum took a quick look around, just to be sure he wasn't walking into an ambush. He had no reason not to trust Carrie, but then again, he wasn't sure what she wanted from him.

"I need to examine their equipment, to record water pressures and flows, to see how much dirt is actually blown off the far side of the gorge. And then I—"

"I'll go with you," Slocum said, stopping her again. "If we get back before tomorrow morning, that is."

Her eyes widened. He wondered if he had ever seen a more beautiful woman. He couldn't remember when.

"It should not take that long. It is only a short ride to the mine. The miners ought to be gone, perhaps only the foreman still there."

Slocum heard loud noises in the street, followed by gun-fire. He pushed Carrie to one side and peered out a broken window. A slow smile crossed his lips.

"No need to worry about Lou Morgan being at the mine. I'd say he's come to town with the rest of the miners and tied one on."

The mine foreman staggered along the street, an empty whiskey bottle in one hand and a smoking six-gun in the other. He repeatedly fired the six-shooter, the hammer now falling every time on an empty chamber. He seemed not to notice the difference between bullets blasting through the still air of Oroville and the hollow click of futile dry-firing.

"So I see," Carrie said. "Can we go to the mine right away? The sooner I do my survey, the sooner I can be on my way."

"Where to? Sacramento?"

The question took the redhead by surprise. She started to answer, closed her mouth as if thinking, then said, "Why, yes, of course, Mr. Slocum. Or may I call you John?"

"That'd be fine." He smiled a little and added, "Carrie." She didn't berate him for the impertinence. Instead she guided him through the dilapidated building and out to an alleyway. "I often used this place for meetings because it was free. However, it has fallen into great disrepair. With the mine closed now, I suppose I can forget about it entirely."

"You sound as if you'd prefer to stay here," Slocum said.

"I get tired moving about. Settling down has never appealed to me before. But now, Oroville is a nice community. All the better because of the hydraulic mine's closing," she added hastily. "But I'd need more reason to remain." She turned her emerald eyes on him, as if he might give her the reason.

"You have a buggy or do you have a horse over at the stable?" asked Slocum.

"A horse. I have a horse. Do you think it is unseemly for me to ride?" she asked, as if accusing him of some crime.

He shrugged. They reached the livery, sounds of more gunfire in the distance. He decided it might be better to leave Oroville for a spell rather than face the wrath of the miners as they got drunker and started protesting their bad fortune. Cinching down his saddle, he turned to help Carrie. She had finished with her saddle and was getting ready to mount. He went to help her. She hesitated a moment, then bent her leg and let him boost her into the saddle.

The feel of her leg set Slocum's heart pounding. From her horse, she looked down and said, "Time to ride."

He nodded and mounted his horse, and the pair of them rode away from Oroville, cutting through the hills and arriving at the mine in far less than an hour. Slocum saw that Carrie rode expertly and was no stranger to rough terrain. They came out of the forest at the end of the huge gorge cut by the hydraulic monitors.

"Those are the shaker tables," Slocum said, pointing out the equipment. "Tons of mud comes gushing down, gets sluiced across the screens, then shaken to bring up all the rocks. Men paw through the rubble and discard the dross. What's left ought to be decent gold-bearing ore, flakes of gold or even nuggets."

Slocum watched the woman closely. She paid little attention to the damage done by the monitors. Instead, she studied the tons of refuse produced by the water cannon. Dismounting, she walked over and picked up a shovel. She dug in the piles until dirt flew like a gopher digging a hole.

"You looking for anything in particular?" Slocum asked, hooking his leg across the pommel of his saddle. Leaning forward, he studied the pile she had made, trying to determine her reason for digging like this.

"Seeing how bad the rock itself has been destroyed," she said. At this he blinked. The entire damned mountain had been cut apart by the torrents of water. Looking at individual rock ripped out of the side of the gorge seemed unnecessary to him.

Seeing his interest in what she did, Carrie tossed down the shovel and studied the sides of the gorge for the first time. "I think we ought to make our way to the camp and study the equipment so I can note how it is all used."

Slocum said nothing as she easily mounted and led the way up the steep bank, past where he had been bush-whacked and along a trail he had not realized even existed.

"You surely do know your way around," he observed.

"I . . . I've been spying on the miners for some time," she said. He wondered why it sounded like a lie when it was probably the truth.

He rode behind the woman, studying her beauty. She rode as if she had been born in the saddle, something he would never have guessed watching her haranguing the crowd in Oroville about the evils of mining. They reached the outskirts of the camp. Carrie immediately slid from the saddle and tethered her horse. She motioned him to silence. He followed her lead, wondering if it might not be simpler if they walked into camp and looked around. Who was likely to stop them?

Certainly not a drunk and disorderly Lou Morgan. Wyoming and the other miners had left. And as far as Slocum knew, he had been the only guard hired on at the mine. He wasn't about to stop Carrie from doing anything she wanted.

"Are the water pumps over here?" she asked, seemingly lost.

"There," Slocum said, frowning. For someone who admitted to spying on the mine, she had little idea where anything was. But down below, at the sluice where the gold was separated, she had not only known her way around the area, but had dug like she meant it in the discarded sludge.

She wandered about, not seeming to know exactly what she wanted. Now and then Carrie stopped and nodded, as if finding precisely the place she wanted, but Slocum saw no reason for any of it. He followed, more interested in watching her as she bent over than in what she was doing.

"I have found enough to report fully," Carrie said, brushing off her hands. She turned and gave him her radiant smile. For a moment, a ray of sunlight hit her face and made her seem to be something more than a mere woman.

Slocum stiffened, crouched, and went into a spin, drawing his Colt Navy in a blindingly fast movement. He fired an instant after the report echoed through the empty mining site. His bullet ripped away boards from Lou Morgan's shack, sending pieces flying in all directions. The slug passed through the wood and into the structure, forcing the sniper with the rifle to duck back inside.

"John, what?" Carrie stood, bewildered.

"We're being shot at," he said, shoving her away. She stumbled and fell to her knees as a second shot whined through the air. This slug went wide too. Slocum began firing at the shack, hoping to flush the ambusher.

"John, wait, don't go. You might be hurt!" cried Carrie.

"Keep your head down," he shouted. He cursed her bright red hair. It made her an easy target. Sending two more slugs into the side of the foreman's shack produced no response. Slocum dropped behind a water pump, reloaded, then went hunting.

Keeping low, he dashed from his cover to the door. Never slowing, he kicked hard, sending the door crashing inward, knocking it off its hinges with a screech of torn wood. Slocum swung around, ready to kill whoever hid inside.

The shack stood empty. His quarry had fled. Slocum found some footprints outside, the prints less sharp now in the drying dirt than they had been the previous day in the mud, but matching those of the bushwhacker who had knocked him into the gorge. Starting after the backshooter, he stopped when he heard Carrie cry out, "John, wait. Don't!"

He turned back to the red-haired woman, worrying she might have run afoul of the owlhoot trying to kill them. She came out, foolishly undaunted by two shots intended to blow off her pretty head.

"Stay down! I don't know where the varmint got off to!" Slocum worried she would flush the sniper, but he heard and saw nothing. Reluctantly, he holstered his pistol, knowing he could never overtake the man now.

"John, I was so scared!" She threw her arms around him and held him close. He moved to keep his gun hand free, then decided the gunman had taken off like a scalded dog and wasn't going to try a second time to kill him.

Or had the bushwhacker been aiming at Slocum at all? He might have been shooting at Carrie. The first shot ought to have gone straight to its target since Slocum had been an instant late understanding the trap and responding. Then he began to forget all logic. Carrie looked up, her green eyes aglow. Her ruby lips parted slightly and her eyelids closed.

He kissed her. And then he forgot completely about gunmen and ambushes and anything other than the feelings growing within his loins. She was a desirable woman—and there was no doubt he had desired her from the minute he set eyes on her.

She kissed him back. Hard. This removed any doubt Slocum might have had about her feelings toward him. She moved against him, her firm breasts pressing into his body.

"Where, John?" she asked. "Where can we go? The foreman's shack?"

"Bunkhouse," Slocum decided. Morgan's cabin was shot full of holes, and he would feel exposed there. As that thought flashed across his mind, he had to smile. More than his backside would be exposed. Already Carrie was opening the front of her blouse, showing the frilly undergarments she wore. A shake of her shoulder, and even this masking cloth sank down, exposing acres of creamy white skin. Almost coyly, she pulled the material away from her breast and let him get a glimpse of the bright red cherry nipple topping it.

"Do you like what you see?" she asked in a husky voice.

"I want more."

"Men," she said in mock anger. "Always so greedy."

"For you." He kissed her lips again, then licked and kissed at her earlobe. This brought forth soft moans of pleasure, but when he worked his mouth to the tops of her breasts, he got real sighs of delight.

He kissed the pointy tip of one breast, then sucked hard on the nub he found there. Carrie almost collapsed. His strong arms supported her as he moved to the other breast and lavished equal attention on it.

"I don't think I can make it to the bunkhouse," she said. "Here. Now. Please, John!"

She ripped open her blouse and cast it aside. She stood naked to the waist, the soft afternoon wind blowing across her sensitive flesh. As warm as the air was, gooseflesh popped up all over her firm breasts. Slocum lavished more kisses on them, then worked lower where Carrie fumbled to get her skirt unfastened.

He didn't help her. He dropped down, his hands slipping under the flare of the material. His hands found the warmth of her legs and stroked upward.

"Oh, yes, John, that feels so good." She shivered and sighed and widened her stance. He stroked up the woman's inner thighs and felt her tremble like a young colt ready to race across a meadow. Seeing what he was doing, she hiked her skirts around her waist, and Slocum knew he had found paradise.

His hand brushed across the fleecy mat he discovered between her legs. Together they sank to the ground. Somehow he got off his gunbelt and unbuttoned his fly. His manhood snapped out, rigidly at attention, a soldier waiting for inspection. Like a thirsty woman grabbing for a cup of water, Carrie seized his rigid length and drew it forward. The tip brushed across the tangled red nest of fur, then slipped into her.

Carrie tensed at the intrusion. Slocum felt as if he had sunk into a mine shaft that threatened to collapse all around him. Hot and moist, she closed around his length. Her legs parted and allowed him to move up, sinking even deeper.

"I love it, John, I love the way you feel, but the rocks! My back!"

Slocum saw the problem. They lay on the approach to the water pumps, and had not bothered even to find a spot cushioned with pine needles or soft dirt. He rolled over, choosing his position the best he could. He ended up beneath her. The woman rose over him. He reached up and cupped her breasts, squeezed them, and began urging her in an up-and-down movement of her hips that gave them both supreme pleasure.

Carrie moaned and sobbed and began rising and falling faster. Slocum's hardened spike of flesh vanished farther and farther into her yearning interior with every drop of her hips. When she started twisting from side to side as well as going up and down, Slocum knew he wasn't going to be able to continue much longer. The desires mounting in his loins were too intense.

"Hurry," he said. "Can't keep going like this too much longer."

"I, yes, I know. Oh, oh!" Carrie's entire body tensed. She threw back her head and cried out loud in ecstasy. Her entire body shivered and shook as waves of desire passed through her. Slocum felt the rock-hard tips of her nipples harden even more as he stroked over them. Then he lost all sense of himself as he shared her sexual fire.

She sank down, their chests pressed together. She laid her cheek against his and sighed softly.

"I never knew it could be like this, John. We make a good couple." Carrie ran her fingertips over his cheek.

Slocum wasn't up to disputing that. He was even less inclined to argue when she did things to him that repeated all they had done—and more.

5

Slocum and Carrie got back to town a little past sundown. She rode close, her leg occasionally bumping into his, reminding them both of their well-spent afternoon at the mine. Slocum found his thoughts meandering to the attack that had started their afternoon and to why anyone would want to kill him—or Carrie Sinclair.

He didn't have any good reason for the attack, other than it had led to more enjoyment than he'd had in a long time. When he had patrolled the gorge rim working for Lou Morgan, there had been reason for bushwhackers to take aim at him. But why shoot now at people poking about a shuttered mine?

He didn't come to any good answers.

"I'd best ride on in by myself, John. In a town this size, tongues do wag." The red-haired woman looked at him, and what he got from that smile curling her lips was a wish for something other than a parting. She impetuously bent over and gave him a quick peck on the cheek. He couldn't help comparing that to the kisses when they had been at the mine. This one did nothing to quell the feelings he had inside. If anything, it inflamed them, as innocent as it seemed.

But he said, "Reckon you're right. Ride ahead. I'll watch the back trail to be sure that owlhoot who potshotted at us doesn't come sneaking around for a second try."

"You're a good man, John Slocum," the redhead said. Then she put her heels to the horse's flanks and rocketed off. Slocum watched her ride. She flowed with the animal. He would not have expected her to be such a fine horseman, and he wasn't sure why he thought that. He knew nothing about her, and Carrie was strangely reticent about revealing much of herself. Whenever she got close to saying something personal, she always backed away like she'd stomped on a rattler and went into one of her tirades about hydraulic mining or some other social cause.

Slocum dismounted at the stable, seeing Carrie's horse had already been put into a stall. He made sure the stable boy would take care of both horses, then went in search of a room for the night. In only one day many miners had left the town. Slocum had seen rats racing out of a deep mine shaft about to be flooded. This wasn't much different. He could have had his choice of deserted cabins dotting the road between Oroville and the mine, but he chose a hotel that looked decent, preferring clean sheets and a soft mattress.

As he lay down and stared at the ornate plaster ceiling, his back ached. Slocum smiled, remembering why his back felt this way. After a spell, he drifted to sleep, awakening only when dawn poked through the thin curtains dangling over the eastern window.

On his way to find a decent breakfast, he saw an ebullient Astin Barclay slapping men on the back and making himself a nuisance. The strange man smiled broadly when he spied Slocum, and rushed across the street to shake his hand like it was a pump handle and he was dying of thirst.

"A good morning to you, Mr. Slocum," greeted Barclay. He dropped his voice a little, but still spoke loud enough

for several of the merchants along the boardwalk to overhear.

"I have had singular good fortune since last we met. I
have discovered even more diamonds!" He pulled a dun-
colored chamois cloth from his coat pocket and held out
the contents so they caught the bright rays of the rising sun.
Against the cloth, they seemed even more dazzling. Slocum
squinted at the brilliant stones. "See? A thousand dollars
worth. More!"

"Where are you getting these?" Slocum asked, thinking
he already knew the answer. He took Barclay's arm and
steered the man away when the interest shown by the men
along the boardwalk became obvious. The owner of the
bookstore seemed particularly fascinated by the open dis-
play of the stones. He chewed his lower lip, then ducked
into his store. Slocum saw him pawing through a stack of
books on the counter until he found one. The man opened
the volume and read a few lines, then looked up to see
Slocum staring at him. Almost like a child caught with his
hand in the cookie jar, the merchant slammed the book shut
and hid it behind his back.

"You are not an unintelligent man, Mr. Slocum. You
surely must know, or at least have a good guess." Barclay
smiled. He pulled Slocum along the street, the diamonds
still resplendent in the sunlight.

"I was on my way to get some breakfast," Slocum said.
"If you haven't eaten, we can talk about getting to San
Francisco."

"Food, yes, a capital idea. There," said Barclay, pointing. "An eating establishment with some promise of decent
victuals." Barclay steered him in the direction of a cafe
where a half-dozen well-dressed men were eating. Barclay
found a table in the middle of them.

They ordered and ate quickly, Barclay chattering on and
on about his great good luck in a whisper that carried

throughout the cafe. Slocum noted how the others turned so they could listen to the conversation, but nothing he said quieted the effusive Astin Barclay.

"Here, my dear lady," he said to the waitress. He handed her one of the stones he had carried in the chamois cloth.

"What is this?" she asked.

"Wealth far in excess of this simple meal's worth," Barclay said, "but your kind smile and swift service deserve more than a few dollars in way of recompense."

"We don't take no ore," she said tartly. "Gold dust or scrip, if you have it. Otherwise, you wash dishes."

"My dear lady!" protested Barclay. "This is worth a king's ransom! Here. Look at it!"

"Don't know about ore," she said almost sullenly. Slocum guessed she was less than enthusiastic about the mine closing and taking with it many of her customers, even if the miners were rude and uncouth for such a decent cafe.

"Find someone who knows," Barclay said. "And this is not mere ore. Look at the surrounding material on this . . . diamond." Heads turned all around. Before, it had been a customer trying to weasel out of paying. Now these successful-looking men were drawn like flies to honey. Slocum sat back, wondering at Barclay's game. Whatever it was, it might not be exactly legal.

Somehow, that didn't bother him too much.

"My husband's out back cooking," the waitress said. "I'll ask him. But don't you go runnin' off now, you hear?"

"I hear you, my dear lady," Barclay replied. He turned to Slocum and said, "It is difficult to be charitable to the lower classes. They seldom allow you to be magnanimous." He rocked back in his chair and folded his hands over his ample belly. The smile on Barclay's face told Slocum his plan, whatever it was, was proceeding well.

The waitress came back and dropped the diamond on the table. "Ned says he don't know what the hell this is. Greenbacks or gold, that's the way you pay or I call the marshal."

"Very well," Barclay said, peeling off bills from a roll of scrip he carried in his coat pocket. He dropped them on the table. With a deft movement, he scooped up the diamond. Acting impetuously, he drew the diamond across the edge of his drinking glass, leaving a long, deep scratch. "There's more than enough to pay for the glass too," Barclay said.

Outside, Slocum asked, "Is it smart showing around those diamonds to everybody? Might cause something of a problem getting to San Francisco. When miners are out of work, some of them are likely to turn to pursuits less than legal, if you catch my drift."

"I do, Mr. Slocum. You are astute, and I am afraid I have allowed my good feelings to get the better of me." Barclay thought for a moment, looking up and down the main street in Oroville like a cat studying a nest of baby birds.

"You ready to leave town?" Slocum asked.

"I . . . I have changed my plans. These changed them," Barclay said, patting his coat pocket where the diamonds bulged prominently. "I was unsure before. Now I am willing to postpone my trip. Keeping you on the payroll, of course," he added hastily.

"You thinking someone might want to shoot you down?" Slocum asked.

"I need assistance, that's all. I feel as safe as a babe in his mama's arms because of my righteousness," Barclay said pompously, "but your presence will contribute greatly to my success. The mine closing has aided my cause immensely."

"What might that cause be?" asked Slocum.

"Ah, wait, there. See that gentleman?" Barclay pointed

at a scruffy prospector shuffling along the dusty street, his long-eared, flea-bitten mule protesting loudly with every step.

"What of him?"

Barclay was already hurrying to the old prospector. The man jumped back, his hand going to a knife shoved into his belt, when Barclay rushed for him. The mule brayed loudly and dug in its heels, not about to move.

"Mr. Webber, isn't it?" Barclay said.

"I'm Webber."

"I wish to conduct business with you."

"Business? What you selling?" the old geezer asked suspiciously. "Whatever it is, I ain't buyin'. Got no money."

"But you own land. I would pay you handsomely for what you own adjacent to the mine."

"That damned hydraulic mine? They chawed up and spit out half my property already. Undercut it, they did, using their water cannon, and the marshal wouldn't do squat about it. Said I had to sue them or something. I don't hold with lawyers, 'less it's to string up the bastards. Like judges even less."

"One thousand dollars," Barclay said.

"How's that? You wantin' me to give you a *thousand* dollars?" Webber brayed like his mule. "I ain't got fifty cents to my name, mister."

"No, no, you do not understand. I want to *buy* your land. We can do a quit claim and in return I shall confer upon you one thousand dollars!"

Webber looked at Barclay like he had gone daft. Slocum shared the opinion. No matter how much land the grizzled old prospector had laid claim to, it wasn't worth such a princely sum. Or was it? Slocum wasn't so sure any longer.

"You been out in the sun too long?" Webber asked. "Eatin' locoweed? Heard tell there was a case of bad tomatoes that dang fool Sarrantonio what runs the store sold.

Tins was ready to bust wide open, they were.'' Webber scratched himself, losing his thought in a cobwebby haze from too much of the very things he accused Barclay of partaking.

"Let's you and I go to the land office and record the transfer,'' Barclay said, taking Webber by the arm. The prospector jerked away, squinted, then saw the greenbacks Barclay flashed. Greed drove him now that he saw Barclay wasn't funning him.

"Show me where to make my mark. That land's well nigh useless for mining, the way they cut out all the good ore from under it.''

"Yes, yes.'' Barclay put his arm around the man's shoulders, his nose twitching in response to the lack of recent bathing. Slocum started to follow, but Barclay waved him away. Slocum understood. Men like Webber weren't used to being in crowds, except when they chose. Living a solitary existence was preferable to having his elbows jostled all the time.

Slocum understood. He felt the same way.

He trailed the pair to the land office. A saloon across the street, undoubtedly getting great business from those registering or selling claims, beckoned to him. He went in, bought a quarter bottle of rotgut, then settled into a chair where he could look out a dusty window and keep the land office across the street in plain view.

He'd finished his first shot when he saw Carrie Sinclair hurrying down the street. She stopped outside the land office, stamped her foot, glanced over her shoulder into the office as if no one would notice, then bulled her way in.

She collided with Astin Barclay on his way out and clutching a sheaf of papers. Webber pushed past them, waving the handful of fluttering greenbacks around like a flag in a Fourth of July parade. He hardly glanced at the lovely red-haired woman as he made his way down the street, cackling like a rooster spotting the first light of day.

Carrie and Barclay stood nose-to-nose on the walk in front of the land office. Slocum couldn't make out their words, but they were arguing. She stamped her foot, then pushed hard against the portly man's chest, pinning him against the wall. Slocum stood and moved to the swinging saloon doors, trying to hear what was going on.

As he got to the point where he might have heard, Carrie spun and stalked off. All he heard were the echoes from her heels clacking against the boardwalk. Slocum faded back into the saloon, wondering what had happened. It looked for the world as if Carrie Sinclair and Astin Barclay had continued a fight that had already started. That meant they knew each other well enough to quarrel.

He returned to the chair and poured a second drink as Barclay came in. Slocum looked up, wondering if Barclay would comment on his brief altercation with Carrie Sinclair.

He didn't.

"Ah, my good man, things go well!"

"You bought his land?"

"At a steal of a price! Now all I need do is find this Henry Emerson fellow and—"

"The Gold Trident's owner?"

"Why, yes," said Barclay, eyebrows rising. "But you worked for him. I forgot!"

"Never met the man, but heard his name bandied about some," Slocum admitted. "I got the impression he wasn't around here. Maybe in San Francisco."

"He is, he is," Barclay said quickly. Too quickly. "I have so much to do before I meet him."

"What needs doing? Anything I can help out with?" asked Slocum, wondering what the answer might be. He felt as if he had dropped his poke on a table, looked around at the other cardplayers, and failed to figure out who the sucker was.

That meant he was the mark.

"Spread the word wherever you go, my good sir." Barclay leaned over and whispered huskily, "I have formed the Great California Land Company with the intent of buying all the land occupied by the mine—and its environs."

"You're buying up everything around the mine?"

"Mum's the word when it comes to my identity. The joy of a company is the ability to hide one's identity from the riffraff. No one need know I am the owner of the Great California Land Company and am doing the purchasing."

Slocum said nothing. Nobody would know, as long as they were deaf and blind and living somewhere in China.

"I must go and tend to pressing business. In a few days, we will leave for San Francisco. You will escort me, of course, and we will track down this Mr. Emerson, and he will fall all over himself to sell me the Gold Trident. Yes, yes," chortled Astin Barclay as he left Slocum with his bottle.

Before Slocum had finished the whiskey, he had decided to make another trip to the mine. He wasn't sure what he was looking for, but it had to be worth at least a thousand dollars for land already gutted by the hydraulic mining.

6

"I've missed you so much," Carrie said, running her fingers up and down his arm as they stood in the street. She gripped a little more firmly and moved closer. Slocum felt the heat of her sleek body and the stirring within him, but all he could do was wonder about the argument she'd had with Astin Barclay the day before. "I thought you'd come by last night." Carrie turned bright emerald eyes up to him.

"Had business," Slocum lied. He wasn't exactly sure why he had not sought her out. Too much was going on that he didn't understand. Until he got a better idea of where he stood, with her and with Barclay, he wanted to play his cards close to the vest.

"Not that old Mr. Barclay, was it? How dare he take you away from me!" She smiled wickedly, and Slocum momentarily forgot what he had been doing.

"You know him, don't you?" he asked.

"Why, yes. He came into town just a little before the mine closed. I asked him for financial support but he—did not give it to me," she said, as if rushing to a conclusion. Slocum knew a lie when he heard one. Carrie was a good liar, but not that good. She hadn't sat in on enough poker games to learn how to fake the truth, or how to recognize the lies of other players.

"You hear about the Great California Land Company?" Slocum asked, taking a shot.

"Barclay's company? Why, yes. He's trying to buy as much land as possible around the old mine."

"He's going to San Francisco to talk turkey with Emerson over buying the entire mine—equipment, gorge, and all."

Carrie didn't seem unduly surprised at this. "He's a cunning man, that Astin Barclay. Don't get tangled up too much with him, John."

"You know about the diamonds he claims to have found? From the way he's acting, it's not much of a secret he thinks the diamonds are in the same dirt that gave up the gold."

"Some men are unable to keep a secret," Carrie said seriously, as if she had just discovered a new truth of the universe. "I'm glad you are able to. My reputation . . ." She sighed, stroking the front of his vest with her long, slender fingers that knew all the right places to touch. "It would be irreparably damaged if anyone figured out that you and I, I mean, that we . . ." She actually blushed as she averted her eyes. Slocum found this fetching.

"Your secret's safe with me. Seems Barclay isn't much at keeping secrets. He's been waving around those diamonds and a wad of money he claims came from the sale of other diamonds."

"Claims?" she asked, frowning. "You think he is lying? Where'd the diamonds come from, then, if not around the old mine?"

"I've heard of clever frauds. All he'd need is a real diamond or two. Not a one of these miners has ever seen a diamond in the rough. They wouldn't know one if it upped and bit 'em."

"Would you?"

"No," Slocum said.

"I would," came the surprising response. "My father was a jeweler, intensely interested in all precious stones. I read his books and listened while he talked with men from South Africa who mined diamonds."

"Do tell," Slocum said, marveling at the coincidence.

"Blue dirt," she said unexpectedly.

"Come again?"

"Blue dirt. A clay where most diamonds are found. We ought to look for it to see if Barclay is really onto something."

"If he is?"

"We can buy into his company! Or better yet, buy up the land from under him. Yes, that's it! I have a few dollars. We can buy the land for ourselves and get the diamonds— or force him to buy the land from us at an immense price!"

Slocum knew greed when he saw it. If it had a color, Carrie would have been drenched in it. It rang in her voice, shone in her green eyes, exuded from her pores like sweat on a hot noonday.

"Don't look to me for money," he said. "I have what I got paid for two nights guard duty at the mine." He touched his shirt pocket. Added to the few coins he had ridden into Oroville with, he might have as much as three dollars left. In addition, he had the money Barclay had given him, but he felt that wasn't earned yet. Hardly enough to become a land tycoon, in any case.

"You play poker, don't you?" she asked, taking another unexpected turn.

"Some."

"I suspect you are a great player. We can get some of the men who own the land surrounding the mine into a game, and you can win their land! They'll think you are a fool wanting worthless land in return for poker winnings. They can't possibly know it has diamonds on it!"

"You're making a lot of suppositions," Slocum said

slowly. "We'd have to assume those who owned the land played poker and would lose to me. Not everyone likes a good hand of cards." He mentally added that some of those who did were better players than he would ever be. And Lady Luck always sat in on every game, and often favored the drunk and the fool over the expert.

"We can do it, John. I am sure of it!"

Slocum saw Barclay swaggering down the street looking like the cat who had found a bowl of cream. He even preened himself like he was wiping cream from his whiskers.

"It ought to be safe for you to get back to the mine and see if you can find this blue clay," Slocum said. "From the way he's walking, I'd say Barclay is determined to find me. I reckon he is ready to ride on into San Francisco and make an offer to Emerson for the mine."

"Stop him! Don't let him gain control this easily! He'll get rich and leave us paupers!"

"What would you want me to do? Put a bullet through him?"

"What?" Carrie's eyes went wide with horror. "No, not that! I'm not saying kill the man. Slow him down. Do what you can to convince Mr. Emerson not to sell, not right away, not until we can make an offer. We need time to raise money for a competing bid."

"You need to find out if diamonds are even out there. I'm not sure Barclay isn't running a con game."

"On whom, John? He's doing all the buying. He's paying out the money."

"He's making you crazy as a bedbug over the notion of buying the land instead," Slocum pointed out. "Find a diamond or two out there, if you know where to look. I'll ride with Barclay to San Francisco, but I doubt much will get done. Emerson isn't going to sell. Not yet."

"How can you be so sure?" Carrie asked.

"Just a feeling," said Slocum. Carrie chewed on her lower lip in consternation, then stood on tiptoe to give Slocum a quick kiss and dashed off before Barclay saw them together. Slocum waited to be discovered by the stout man. In an hour they were on the trail for San Francisco.

"So good of you to come along with me, Mr. Slocum," said Barclay. The portly man rubbed his hands together, almost dropped the buggy reins, and hastily grabbed them again when the horse felt the lack of control.

"You're wound up tighter than a two-dollar watch," Slocum observed.

"It's the trip, my good man. San Francisco. Henry Emerson. I can get the land from him. What does he want with a mine that's petered out?"

"He might figure you found more gold there."

"But Miss Sinclair and the others would prevent gold mining."

"Hydraulic mining. Don't think many of the out-of-work miners would object much to dropping a mine shaft. Reckon the people of Oroville would welcome that, no matter what Carrie Sinclair said. The objection was to ripping away hundreds of tons of dirt to get to the gold, not actually mining it."

"Hmm, you are right, of course. I need a story why I want the land."

"Why do you? Diamonds?" asked Slocum.

Barclay looked suddenly cagey. "I never said I got the diamonds there, now did I?"

"Reckon not, but you've paid out a powerful lot of money for land surrounding the Gold Trident Mine."

"I know how to make a fortune," Barclay said with some satisfaction. His head began rotating like a lighthouse beacon. "I've done it many times. This time I intend to hang on to what I make."

Slocum reached over and unfastened the leather thong across the hammer of his Colt Navy. Barclay was acting strangely, and Slocum felt the hairs on the back of his neck beginning to rise. He had long since learned to heed the warning of impending havoc. Whether it came from long experience or some sixth sense, he neither knew nor cared.

His six-shooter cleared leather, and Slocum got off a shot before he even realized he was acting. The slug ricocheted off the rock where the road agent lay prone, tore up some shards, and momentarily blinded the man with the rock dust. Slocum had hoped to at least wing him. He fired a second shot. This one drove the startled bandit down the far side of the rock and out of sight.

"What's wrong?" demanded Barclay. He sat up like a prairie dog, his head twisting this way and that and his nose working as if he sniffed the air for danger.

"Get moving. I'll cover you."

Slocum galloped ahead. He fired twice more at a second highwayman who came into view on the far side of the boulder. Like the first, this one seemed shocked that they had drawn fire without even getting off a shot of their own. The pair of bandits huddled together, giving Slocum a clean shot at them. He took it. One yelped in pain and grabbed at his right arm.

To Slocum's surprise, this was enough to run them both off. They hightailed it through a tumble of rocks. Slocum considered going after them, then reined back. It wasn't his place to capture or kill them. His job was to see that Astin Barclay reached San Francisco without getting ventilated— or having the stones hidden away in the chamois cloth stolen.

Galloping almost a half mile allowed him to overtake the fleeing Barclay. The portly man reined back, giving his lathered horse a needed rest.

"What happened? Why were you shooting?"

"You didn't see them? A pair of highwaymen laid a trap for you. I chased them off."

"D-did you injure them?" Barclay's eyes fixed on the smoking six-shooter in Slocum's steady grasp. Slocum took a few minutes to reload and thrust the six-gun back into the cross-draw holster.

"Not enough," Slocum answered at length. He heaved a sigh. He had seen inept robbers before, but none so ill-prepared as this pair. Going after them to pry loose the details of what they had hoped for might be interesting, but Slocum's curiosity led him in other directions. Toward San Francisco with Astin Barclay.

"Been a while since I saw San Francisco," Slocum said. They bobbed gently on the ferry from Oakland heading toward the distant docks across San Francisco Bay. His horse neighed at the unusual shifting caused by the waves breaking at the mouth of the Bay coming all the way from far-off China.

He gentled both his and Barclay's horse, turning from the city toward the corpulent man hunched over in his buggy. Slocum tried to figure out Barclay and couldn't. A strange blend of anticipation, excitement, and maybe apprehension filled the man.

Then the mood dissolved like fog over the water. Barclay straightened, and he was again the ebullient, confident man he had been in Oroville.

"Yes, sir, Mr. Slocum, there lies destiny. Riches. Wealth beyond compare."

"You figure to approach Emerson straightaway?" Slocum asked.

"No, no, I need to verify my find." Barclay patted his coat pocket with the chamois cloth filled with stones. "I shouldn't think it would be difficult to find a banker able to appraise these fine stones."

"Banker? What do they know, besides counting other people's money?" asked Slocum. "You want an expert. A jeweler."

"Why, yes, of course. I am so glad you are accompanying me, my good man. My enthusiasm is blurring my good sense."

Slocum didn't comment on that. The ferry banged into the dock, and in a few minutes they were riding through the bustling streets of the prosperous city. Since the '49 Gold Rush, San Francisco had done nothing but grow and prosper. Even the Panic of '73 had not seriously hurt the merchants there. Shipping from the Orient, increasing travel up and down the Pacific coast, and the completion of the Transcontinental Railroad had all infused vast torrents of money into the city's pockets.

As they rode through Portsmouth Square, Barclay jumped to his feet in the buggy, spooking his horse with the impetuous move. "There!" he cried. "A jeweler, as you suggested, Mr. Slocum."

Slocum took a few seconds to locate the dingy-fronted shop nestled down an alley. How Barclay had spotted it was beyond him. They tethered their horses, and Slocum followed a half-running Barclay into the small shop.

For a jeweler's, the shop had little in the way of merchandise, but the graying man sitting at a bench had a full set of jeweler's tools arrayed around him. The way he expertly peered at the stone Barclay silently handed him told Slocum the man was knowledgeable.

He watched as the jeweler turned the raw stone over and over, peering at it through his magnifying loupe. He took a sharp-pointed instrument and gently dislodged some of the rock from around the stone, then peered at both the part cracked off and the stone itself. He muttered something Slocum did not quite understand about "blue clay," then rocked back in his chair, placing the stone on a green felt pad between him and Barclay.

"An insignificant diamond, sir," said the jeweler. "However, you have more than an ample supply, I would say." He dropped the loupe, rocked back on the chair's rear two legs, and put on half-glasses, eyeing the lump in Barclay's coat pocket.

"You mean the diamond's no good?" asked Slocum.

"It's not the finest quality," the jeweler said, peering at Slocum over the top of his half-glasses. He settled in his chair, all four legs firmly on the floor now. "It's not the most valuable stone I've ever seen, but it *is* a diamond."

"How much?" demanded Barclay. "How much for all these?" He cast out the contents of the chamois cloth onto the counter with a rattle. The jeweler's eyes widened slightly. He pawed through the heap, poking at them to be sure they were of the same quality as the first he had examined.

"A few thousand perhaps," the jeweler said, a sudden slyness in his voice. "No more."

"A hundred thousand?" asked Barclay.

Slocum recognized the ploy. The jeweler had offered a fraction of what the stones were worth. For the first time, Slocum thought Astin Barclay might have a chance at riches.

"I don't have that kind of money." The jeweler made a deprecating motion as he indicated his humble shop. "Give me a few days. Perhaps I can assemble a few men of more prosperous means to—"

"Never mind," said Barclay. "Thank you for your expertise. Keep that stone for your trouble." Barclay pointed to the one the jeweler had originally examined.

"Wait, these diamonds. They were found in California?"

"Why, yes."

"I don't have much money, but if there are more, I can,

I mean, I will—'' The old man seemed flustered for a moment, then settled his thoughts. "I would buy into the mine. You will need a knowledgeable marketeer for the diamonds. For a small share, I can guarantee top price from any buyer.''

"Hmm,'' said Barclay, a slow grin coming to his lips. "A splendid idea. You *would* work more diligently if you owned part of the mine, wouldn't you?''

Slocum slipped out, leaving the two haggling over the price. From outside he heard the jeweler agree to a thousand shares in Barclay's Great California Land Company. Slocum shook his head. The land company had no value— so far.

Unless Henry Emerson sold the petered-out gold mine, Barclay had nothing to barter with. That didn't seem to stop him from offering shares in his company, though. He emerged from the shop, grinning broadly.

"A capital deal, this one, Mr. Slocum. I have a dedicated co-owner now working for both our interests.''

"What now?''

"To a bank for a safe place to hold these fine diamonds, then to a hotel for some much-needed rest. Mr. Ralston's Grand Hotel on Market Street perhaps. No,'' Barclay said, wrestling with his greed and newfound wealth. "Nothing less than the sybaritic luxury of Ralston's Palace Hotel across the street from the Grand will do! And then a night on the town. My treat, Mr. Slocum, for your competent shepherding of the diamonds this far.''

Slocum shook his head, but wasn't going to turn down a night at the Palace Hotel.

7

The sheer opulence of the Palace Hotel made Slocum suck in his breath and hold it. He wasn't dressed for this kind of place, but it hardly seemed to matter to Astin Barclay. He swept into the plushly carpeted lobby as if he were the Pasha of Rajipoor, giving his benediction left and right to any who would slow down to stare at him. Slocum trailed behind, uneasy at having his gear carried by two men dressed like Union Navy admirals.

"The best rooms for my friend and me," Barclay declared loudly. "We will be staying a few days only and require all amenities possible."

As Barclay and the room clerk worked out the arrangements, Slocum looked around the lobby. Sculptures of marble and jade stood everywhere, with oil paintings on the walls. Thick velvet drapes deadened the sound from outside along Market Street, and Slocum had not seen so many men and boys in uniform since the war. By the time they rode the elevator to the third floor and he saw his room, he was ready to believe Astin Barclay had found the mother lode.

"Be ready to go carousing, Mr. Slocum," Barclay said expansively. "My thirst is immense, and I would gamble. Are you a cardplayer? Yes, my good man, I can see you are."

"There's a bank down the street that looks like a mighty fine resting place for your . . . friends," Slocum said, looking significantly at the bulge in Barclay's pocket.

"Yes, yes, of course. But I would keep one as a good-luck charm." Barclay made a show of fumbling through the stones in front of the bellboys until he found the one the jeweler had examined so carefully. Slocum recognized it from the way the surrounding dross had been freshly chipped away to reveal the dull white stone.

A bath, food delivered to his room, and a few minutes lying on the down mattress restored Slocum's vitality even as it piqued his curiosity even more. Barclay showed a strange combination of brilliance and stupidity. He haggled well to get good prices, then showed his hoard to anyone caring to look at it. Flashing the diamonds in front of the bellboys guaranteed word of the man's riches would echo across San Francisco like a cannon shot.

Slocum couldn't understand it. If Henry Emerson caught wind of the diamond find, probably on or near his abandoned hydraulic mine, the price for the Gold Trident would explode. Barclay was shrewd enough to know such extravagance as he showed now would drive up the price Emerson wanted—if the gold mine owner would even sell.

Slocum couldn't figure any way Barclay could come out ahead if Emerson refused to sell, unless Barclay knew something hidden to everyone else. Was Emerson in such a position that he had to sell the mine? He had taken out a fair amount of gold. It had not been a fabulously rich mine, but enough gold had been found to make the high-pressure water cannon and the rest of the operation profitable.

He shook off such idle speculation. It was time to go out on the town with Barclay. Slocum had no fancy clothes to wear, so he satisfied himself with his clean, if shabby, trail clothes. He settled his Colt Navy at his left hip, wondering if the big-city policemen had enacted laws against carrying a six-shooter in public. He would find out. Slocum knew the gangs that had ravaged the city years earlier, the Sydney Ducks among them, were mostly gone—replaced by other equally vicious gangs. Slocum had even heard tell of Chinese tongs controlling crime with an iron fist along Dupont Gai.

He left the room, looking back almost longingly at its luxury. A flash of regret hit him. Too bad Carrie Sinclair wasn't here with him. He collected Astin Barclay, and the pair of them set off toward the bank down the street, where Barclay left most of the stones in a safety box. Slocum heaved a sigh seeing the box slide into the vault, even if the remaining diamond, the one Barclay carried "for luck," might be worth enough to get both their throats slit.

"To somewhere that we can indulge in a fine Delmonico steak," Barclay said. He snapped his fingers and summoned a passing horse-drawn carriage. Slocum found himself uneasy at being a passenger rather than a driver, but held down the feelings. His eyes roved constantly, looking for danger that wasn't present. He finally settled down and relaxed a mite.

After a fine dinner where Barclay did everything but go from table to table showing the other customers the diamond, he and Slocum went back outside and Barclay declared, "To the Barbary Coast. I would see where the lower element lives. And wet my whistle too. It's been a spell since I had whiskey—or much else." Barclay smiled and winked broadly.

"That section of town is a good place to get your throat slit," Slocum said. "Anything on the other side of the fire-lookout tower on Telegraph Hill is sailors' territory."

"I need recreation, my good man," Barclay said. "Come along. I have you to watch my back. What more do I need? After all, luck is riding on my shoulder!" He patted the coat pocket where he carried the diamond, laughed, and

strutted off to the north. Slocum wished Barclay would re-
consider. The way the man spent money, he might as well
go to the Union Club. While he was likely to be separated
from all his money there, it would be more genteelly done,
and there wasn't likely to be blood running on the floor
afterward.

"There are a few places I've heard of," Slocum started.

"The Barbary Coast," Barclay insisted.

"Why not go back to the Palace and rest?" Slocum suggested. "You want to have a clear head when you talk to
Emerson. He might not be as willing to sell the mine as
you think."

"He'll *beg* me to take that worthless land off his hands.
Trust me. I know the rich and how they think. He is even
as we speak looking for someone he considers a sucker to
foist off all that 'worthless' land on." Barclay laughed.
"He will be giving up the wealth of Croesus when he does.
His loss, my gain!"

Slocum couldn't deter the man from heading into the
center of trouble. Deadfalls lined the alleys, women coming
out of cribs and bagnios to proposition drunken sailors and
miners too stupid to realize they might end up floating facedown in the Bay with the dawn tide. The policemen, the
"Specials," walked in pairs and more, islands of relative
law in a sea of total depravity.

Slocum might have enjoyed himself there if it had not
been for Barclay and the way he flashed his wad of greenbacks.

"This one," Barclay said. "A fine place, if I am any
judge."

"You're not," Slocum muttered. The Cobweb Palace
was situated at the end of a long dock, and stepping into
the smoky room told Slocum the derivation of its name.
No section was left uncluttered with filmy spiderwebs.
Above the curving hardwood bar circled a brightly colored

parrot, cursing in three languages Slocum recognized and several more he didn't.

"Whiskey," Slocum shouted over the din to the barkeep. The man lacked an eye. The fox fur patch covered the empty socket—almost.

"Not seen you gents in here before," the bartender said. "Rule of the house. You got to buy one for the parrot." He put three shot glasses on the bar, filling all three. Slocum noted how the end one away from him and Barclay was the fullest.

Before he could say a word, the parrot swooped down, skidded to a halt, and grabbed the shot glass in its powerful beak. A quick jerk brought the glass up. Slocum blinked in amazement as the parrot downed most of the liquor, spilling only a little on its brightly feathered breast. Then it wobbled and fell onto its side. Slocum could have sworn the bird hiccupped.

"Ever see the like before?" Slocum asked of Barclay. He turned, and the man was gone. In a single smooth motion, he had his six-gun out, cocked, and thrust under the barkeep's chin.

"Where'd he go?"

"I—" The man's single eye looked in the direction of a small side door. A cool wind blew through the partly opened portal, coming off the Bay.

Slocum left his whiskey on the bar and rushed to the door, hesitating before he went through. He took a deep breath and almost gagged. Mixed with dead fish and salt-water came a heavy odor of human sweat and urine. He kicked hard on the door, slamming it back on its hinges. His caution was rewarded with a loud cry of pain.

Slocum jumped through, his six-shooter leveled on the man lying in wait behind the door.

"Where's the man you kidnapped?" he asked.

"Dunno what—" The man shrieked in fear as Slocum

discharged the Colt Navy. The bullet ripped off the top of the man's ear.

"There. Down there! We was gettin' paid fifty dollars to recruit a crew! Shanghai!"

Slocum drove his left fist up to the forearm in the man's rock-hard belly. The sailor dropped to his knees, then toppled over, unconscious. Slocum was already on his way down a narrow flight of steps leading to a piling where two men struggled with Astin Barclay. Seeing what was going on, Slocum never hesitated. He fired twice, both bullets blowing away chunks of the rowboat's bottom. In a flash, the men were ankle-deep in water as the boat began sinking.

"Stay there," Slocum ordered, his six-shooter giving authority to his command. He grabbed Barclay's coat collar and pulled him to the bottom step.

"We cain't swim, mister! We cain't!" wailed one scruffy sailor.

"Learn," Slocum said. The way he held his six-shooter told them they could either tread water or die with a .31 slug in their guts. They thrashed about and made their way to the far end of the dock. Slocum let them go.

"Wha—?" Barclay struggled to get his senses back. "My head! What happened?"

"They slugged you. If I hadn't been quick about it, you'd be enjoying the sights of China."

"The Celestial Kingdom? But I—oh," said Barclay, realizing at last the close shave he'd had. His hand went to his coat pocket. A horrified expression crossed his face. "The diamond! It's gone. The other one. The third man. He took it! I tried to stop him but the other two, they, oh, how did this happen?"

"You were stupid," Slocum said harshly. "Be glad you didn't lose more than that stone."

"You don't understand, Slocum! I *have* to have it. I have to get it back!"

"You've got other diamonds in the bank vault worth as much, if not more." Slocum hauled the man up the steep saltwater-soaked steps. By the time they reached the side door into the Cobweb Palace, the man Barclay had accused of stealing his diamond had vanished. A thin trail of blood showed that his wound still bled. Otherwise, he had faded into the crowd inside the bar.

"Please, Mr. Slocum, get it back. Track him down, and get it back. I *have* to have it. I . . . I will give you a tremendous reward."

"Let it lie, Barclay," Slocum said. "This isn't the kind of place to ask questions without attracting attention neither of us could handle."

"Slocum, five thousand shares of stock. In the Great California Land Company. No, not enough, I know, I'll make it ten thousand! Please!"

"What?" Slocum blinked at the offer.

"You'll be rich beyond avarice. Get the diamond back. Hurry, hurry!"

"I'll get you back to the hotel and—"

"I can get back by myself." Barclay shook like a wet dog. Some water had soaked into his fancy duds as he had lain in the rowboat. "I can do that much, Mr. Slocum. Get the diamond back. Please."

Slocum wasn't sure why he agreed. He walked out of the saloon with Barclay, then slowly paced to the end of the dock and saw Barclay into a cab that looked safe enough. He paid little attention as the cab rattled off. He was too busy studying the cobblestone street. He followed a trail of fresh blood—from the man he had shot, he hoped. Too many fights produced too much fresh blood for him to be sure, but the time had been short and he was feeling lucky.

And confused. He couldn't make any sense out of why Barclay was in such a dither over the diamond. The portly man walked around with a pocket filled with them. Any one might be valuable, but was it worth ten thousand shares of stock in his mining company? Slocum decided to find out.

He saw a tiny spot of blood gleaming darkly in the street on a cobblestone under a gas lamp. Then he had to guess where the man he had shot might have gone. The intersection was too busy for Slocum to be certain where to go. He studied each of the three directions and shook his head.

He turned at a sound behind him. An urchin stood there, dirty face staring up at him. He read the cunning in the boy's expression—and he recognized a youngster living by his wits.

"You're lookin' for him, ain't you, mister?"

"Who?"

"Dogmeat," the boy said, then bit his lower lip, as if he had given away too much. Before he could deny anything he'd said, Slocum reached into his shirt pocket and drew out a shiny silver cartwheel. He rolled it along the back of his fingers so it caught the light from the gas lamp.

"Where can I find him?"

"The silver dollar first," the boy said. He grabbed and caught it as Slocum flipped it. Even faster than the boy's hand snaring the coin was Slocum's grabbing the boy's arm when he tried to dart away. Slocum lifted the thin boy off his feet and held him at arm's length.

"This Dogmeat. Did he have a piece of his ear shot off?"

The boy's eyes dropped to the ebony-handled six-gun in Slocum's holster, then boldly stared at him.

"Down the street, an alley, down into the basement of the China-American Trading Company. Building's abandoned."

"Anyone likely to be there with him?"

"You're asking a powerful lot for a lousy dollar," the boy retorted.

Slocum let him down, but did not release his grip. He pulled the boy along behind him until he found the building. The dark alley showed an even darker set of stairs leading down to the building's basement as the boy had claimed.

"Be careful, mister," the boy said when Slocum let him go. "There's always more 'n one snake in every nest." With that piece of street advice, he hightailed it, battered shoes pounding hard against the hard street.

Slocum took a few minutes to reload his six-shooter. This time he had six beans in the cylinder instead of letting his hammer ride on an empty chamber. He cautiously went down the steps and pressed his hand against the wood door he found. It opened on surprisingly well-oiled hinges. Beyond lay nothing but intense darkness.

Taking his time, Slocum slid into the cellar, back pressed against the cold stone wall. Letting his eyes adapt revealed shades of gray within the room. And a door on the far side with a sliver of flickering yellow light oozing out from under like some sickly puddle of melted butter. On cat's feet Slocum crossed the room until he could press his ear against the splintery door panel.

". . . shot my damned ear off! I deserve more 'n one share."

"Shaddup," came a gruff voice. "You know the rules, Dogmeat. The boss gets half, we split the rest of what you steal. And since you let the galoot they was shanghai'n get away, we're out fifty dollars from Cap'n Drago."

Dogmeat grumbled, but soon subsided. Slocum listened hard, and guessed there were at least three men in the room. Dogmeat and his boss plus one other who grumbled but said nothing. Slocum drew his six-gun and pushed open the door a crack. Something gave him away.

The rush of feet caused Slocum to move like lightning. He threw open the door and fired without even knowing what his target might be. A man the size of a small mountain grunted and dropped a sawed-off Meteor shotgun. This was the boss, and he was out of action permanently. Dogmeat and the other hoodlum grabbed for knives.

Slocum turned his Colt Navy on them and said in a cold voice, "Want to join him? I doubt if it's heaven he went to."

The ratlike man beside Dogmeat flipped his wrist, sending his knife cartwheeling through the air. Slocum fired again, this shot catching the man in the leg. He fell like he had been poleaxed.

"You done shot me! It hurts!"

"I'll make it stop hurting, if you want," Slocum said, pointing his six-shooter directly at the man. The whining thug shut up immediately.

"What do you want? You ain't got no call shootin' us up like this. You ain't the law, are you?" demanded Dogmeat. His hand moved to his shot-off ear.

"Where's the rock you took off the man you tried to shanghai?" Slocum asked.

"I don't know what you—ouch!" Dogmeat grabbed his other ear. Slocum's bullet had ripped part of the lobe off. "You're disfigurin' me."

"I ought to make you pay for how I'm improving your looks," Slocum said. "The rock. Where is it?" He lifted his six-shooter again, and this time the muzzle pointed smack between Dogmeat's eyes.

"There! There! He's got it. Had it." Dogmeat pointed to the dead boss. Slocum made his way around the rude table, took the sawed-off shotgun and trained it on the two men, then patted down the dead man's pockets. A lump in his shirt pocket told Slocum where the rock was. He ripped off the pocket. The diamond tumbled into his grip.

"You ain't got no reason to gun us down, mister," complained Dogmeat, not sure which ear to clutch. Both bled.

"Civic improvement," Slocum said coldly. He lifted the shotgun. Both Dogmeat and his comrade in crime scuttled for a hole bored into the dirt floor, vanishing like the rats they were.

Slocum tossed the shotgun aside and retraced his steps through the cellar and onto the street outside the abandoned warehouse. He made certain he had Barclay's precious stone in his pocket, then walked slowly back to the intersection where the urchin had told him about the cellar. The boy was nowhere to be seen. This didn't surprise Slocum. The ragamuffin probably stole from drunks or worked at learning some other disreputable trade. Nothing else could be expected from someone living in the middle of the Barbary Coast.

Slocum passed brothels and dance halls, and slowly worked his way out of the area. He felt dirty and disgusted, and wasn't sure he had risked his life for any good reason. He took out the stone and held it up to the light, watching the unpolished facets reflect brightly.

"So much trouble for this stone," he mused. Slocum pulled out his watch, and was surprised to find his misadventures had taken most of the night. It would be dawn in another hour. Curiosity again dictated Slocum's course of action.

It took him more than an hour to wend his way through the streets back to Union Square. A few shops were already open. He sought out a jeweler—a different jeweler from the one Barclay had sought out the day before.

He tapped lightly on the window of the shop, then held up the diamond to get the man's attention. A short, small man sporting a European-style goatee came to the door and made shooing motions. Slocum held the diamond out for the man to see better. This got the door open.

"I need an appraisal done, if you can." Slocum handed the small man the stone.

"Unusual," the man said, frowning. "This is not the country for raw diamonds. I deal in gold and silver." He scowled as he held out the rock, then went to his workbench and examined it under his loupe. The jeweler dropped his loupe and turned back to Slocum. "So?"

"So, is it real?" Slocum asked.

"Why, yes, of course it is. A diamond in the rough, of course it is."

"What's it worth?"

"Worth?" The man's eyebrows rose and then worked like caterpillars with a hotfoot. His chin quivered a little before he answered. "A few hundred dollars. With proper cutting, perhaps a thousand dollars. It is a flawed stone. It has inclusions, it is slightly yellow, it—"

"Never mind," Slocum said. "This diamond is real and worth as much as a thousand?"

"Perhaps two. I could not say. No one could, until the stone is properly cut. I know only one or two men in California capable of such work. They come from Europe, of course."

"Of course," Slocum said dryly. He picked up the diamond and tucked it back into his pocket. "What do I owe you?"

"Owe me? Answers and nothing more. Where did this diamond come from?"

"Could it be from around here?"

The jeweler's eyebrows did their fuzzy dance again. "Unusual, but possible, perhaps. It is not a spectacular stone, so perhaps it could be from this country. I have heard of a few such diamonds, but . . ." He shrugged eloquently. "Where was this unearthed?"

"Would you buy into a mine producing stones of this quality?"

''Yes,'' the man said too fast. Greed showed under his bushy eyebrows now. ''That would be a good chance to make a . . . few dollars,'' he finished lamely, as if trying to hide his earlier enthusiasm.

''I'll let you know,'' Slocum said, leaving the shop. He made his way to Market Street and the Palace Hotel, where Astin Barclay waited for him. Seldom had Slocum seen a man as relieved as when he gave Barclay the diamond.

8

"Too bad about not finding Emerson," Slocum said. They stood outside the mining magnate's office off Union Square. It had taken almost an hour before they found someone willing to admit Henry Emerson had left San Francisco a few days earlier. No one seemed to know where Emerson had gone, but everyone solemnly assured Slocum it had to be for business reasons. Mr. Emerson never went anywhere for pleasure.

A few discreet inquiries of others in the building who did not work for Emerson had confirmed this devotion to pursuing money for its own sake. Slocum had not located anyone who remembered Emerson taking so much as two days in a row off for vacation. Money drove him, not pleasure.

"If he's not doing business, that means he's not selling the mine," Astin Barclay rationalized. Slocum started to point out all they had learned about Emerson, then bit it back. Let Barclay keep his fantasy alive a little longer. If anything, the man seemed more vital and alive after finding Emerson was not available to sell his mine. The challenge excited him, not the actual doing, or so it appeared to Slocum. He couldn't figure anything else to explain Barclay's

attitude at losing out on tucking the deed to the closed
hydraulic mine into his bank vault next to the diamonds.

"What now?" Slocum asked.

"Back to Oroville, of course. We have land to purchase,
my good man. All around the Gold Trident Mine are small
tracts of land going begging."

"You intending to fetch your diamonds from the bank?"
Slocum asked.

"They are safe there. And I have my lucky stone." Barclay reached into his vest pocket and withdrew the diamond
Slocum had risked his life to retrieve from the shanghaiers.
"This reminds me, Mr. Slocum. I promised you this." Barclay fumbled in a side coat pocket and pulled out a legal
document. He glanced at it, smiled broadly, then handed it
to Slocum.

Slocum's eyes scanned down the elaborately engraved
sheet. He looked up at Barclay, who smiled his cat-licking-
cream smile.

"Ten thousand shares in the Great California Land Company for your fine service so far," said Barclay. "You will
be quite rich when the diamond mine begins operation."

"What if Emerson gets wind of this and decides to mine
the diamonds himself? You must figure most of the diamond deposit is on Emerson's property or you wouldn't be
so eager to get the mine from him."

"Perhaps you should not know too much of the location
I suspect as being the primary source of *our* newfound
wealth," said Barclay, turning conspiratorial.

"Why not? Don't I own ten thousand shares in your
company?" Slocum rattled the ornate stock certificate.

"You do, you do, my good sir, but it will be worth ever
so much more when I complete my purchases! Emerson
must be brought around to sell, of course, but it isn't of
immediate concern since so much else needs to be done.
Back to Oroville!"

Slocum shrugged, then put the stock certificate into his pocket. He had intended to keep riding, maybe up to Oregon to see if he could find some of their fine Appaloosas to train and resell. Timbering in Washington might also provide a summer's work. He had even heard tell of gold finds north in Alaska. Wyoming had mentioned this, and the notion appealed to Slocum.

It took him a few seconds to make up his mind. He followed Barclay back to Oroville—and Carrie Sinclair.

Slocum couldn't believe his eyes. When he had left Oroville, the town had been moribund, and its citizens surly over the closing of the hydraulic gold mine. Now wagons laden with supplies rumbled down the street, kicking up clouds of dust in their rush to deliver their loads. More men walked across the street in front of Slocum than he could remember seeing since first riding in. The merchants seemed to be doing a land-office business—and the land office had a line running around the small shack holding all the recorded deeds.

"Something's happened," Slocum said to Barclay. He watched the rotund man for some reaction. He expected exasperation or irritation, or even fear that a plot of land might elude his Great California Land Company. Barclay's lack of response came as more of a surprise than if he had shouted and ranted or even laughed at what had to be bad fortune.

"We should see what is stirring them up. Let's ask over there," he said, pointing to the land office. They walked to the office.

"Hey, no cuttin' into line. We all got a right to put in our claims," a roughly dressed man said, shoving Slocum back. He wore canvas miner's pants and a torn red-and-black-checked flannel shirt in spite of the day's heat. The man's chin and a razor were strangers, and Slocum's nose wrinkled the closer he got. Bathwater and soap were more than strangers; they were completely alien to this fellow.

"What's the fuss over?" asked Slocum.

"You jist fall off the hay wagon?" the man asked, laughing. His teeth were black and the front one was broken. "You ain't heard about Old Lady Rasmussen and what she found?"

"What was that, good sir?" Barclay asked in a completely neutral voice.

"She chopped the head off a turkey to fix it for dinner, and she found a *diamond* in its crop. A goddamn *diamond*!"

"What does lining up here have to do with a turkey?" Slocum asked.

"We're buyin' land all around her spread. There's got to be tons of diamonds out there!"

Barclay took Slocum by the arm and steered him away. "We must act quickly," he said. "The entire town is ablaze with news of another diamond find. I had hoped to keep the presence of the sparkling wonders a secret, but now . . ." He shook his head and spread his hands in a gesture of complete hopelessness.

"There's still Emerson's mine. He might not know what's going on here," Slocum said.

"True, true, but there is something more to check out. Come along, will you, Mr. Slocum?" Barclay strode off, heading for the general store down the street. A small knot of people crowded about the door into the store.

"What's happening here?" Slocum wondered aloud.

"I remembered that Mrs. Rasmussen's brother-in-law owns this mercantile establishment." Barclay brushed off his clothing and went up the steps, pushing through the gathering. An old woman sat at a small table with a big rock on the table in front of her. Those lining up might have been supplicants worshiping at this rude altar.

"This the so-called diamond?" asked Barclay. He picked up the stone, over the old woman's protests. Barclay held it up, squinted at it, then held it in a thin ray of sunlight coming through a dirty window. He dragged the stone across the glass. A screech sounded—but the window glass did not score.

"This seems suspicious," Barclay said. He put the rock back on the table, sniffed, and declared, "Everyone knows real diamond cuts glass."

"You sayin' this isn't a diamond?" asked someone in the crowd.

"See for yourself." Barclay looked around, grabbed a hammer, and brought it down on the rock. It shattered into a thousand pieces. "Doesn't test all that durable either."

"She didn't find no diamond. She was lyin'!"

"Wait, wait, my good man," said Barclay, interposing his portly body between the angry man and Mrs. Rasmussen. "There are many minerals that, to the untrained eye, appear to be diamonds in the rough. This poor lady was merely wrong, not lying."

Slocum watched the crowd to be sure they didn't turn ugly. They were angry and disappointed, but not dangerous. Then a new ripple passed through as others rushed over from the land office. The big miner Slocum had spoken to earlier roughly shoved to the front.

Belligerently thrusting out his chest, he shouted, "I spent a hunnerd dollars on a claim. I ain't gonna lose my money over no drossy hunk of rock!"

"Sir, be calm," Barclay said. "I'll purchase your claim. One hundred dollars, you said? Here. Here is one hundred ten dollars. You have made a profit."

"Me too, me too!" went up the cry from those in the crowd who had registered land.

"May I?" Barclay sat down next to Mrs. Rasmussen, who looked confused, and started writing quit claims as fast as he could take the deeds. Slocum tried counting how much Barclay spent for the land, and lost track after almost a thousand dollars.

He slipped from the store, and immediately saw Carrie Sinclair. She stood across the street, gesturing frantically to him.

He went to her.

"John, I'm so glad I found you. Have you heard?"

"About Mrs. Rasmussen? Barclay said the rock wasn't a diamond."

"No, no, not that. Two prospectors were out at the edge of the mine. They found all this." She opened a bag filled with small stones. Slocum took one and held it up. It wasn't bright and shining like a diamond, but Slocum knew he was comparing the rock with a cut, polished diamond. He drew it across the glass window behind Carrie.

It left a shallow groove.

"Might be a diamond," he allowed, "but I've heard tell other stones score glass too. All this proves is that it is harder than glass, not that it's a diamond."

"Then let's find out, John. We can go to San Francisco, get an expert evaluation, then we will know for certain."

Slocum considered what she suggested. He wasn't sure Barclay had found any diamonds in the area, but Carrie's bag of stones might confirm a real find. It could mean the difference between a worthless stock certificate in his pocket and something worth a fortune.

Slocum found Astin Barclay amenable to remaining alone in Oroville for a few days. Barclay busily purchased land from any who would tender to him, including Mrs. Rasmussen. He needed neither help nor protection, as long as he kept the people of Oroville happy. Slocum rode with Carrie back to San Francisco to settle the matter of the diamonds once and for all.

• • •

San Francisco began to look familiar to Slocum, like a friend he hadn't seen in ... days. This time, however, he felt better with Carrie riding alongside than he had with Astin Barclay. They rode down Market Street from the ferry. The red-haired woman looked this way and that, as if she had never been in a big city before.

"There, John, there is a jeweler's shop."

Slocum usually covered surprise well. This time his eyebrows rose and his mouth opened. He checked himself before he said a word. Carrie had unerringly found the same jeweler used by Barclay only days earlier. The shop was out of the way and not that well marked. It might have been coincidence, but Slocum wasn't sure he believed in such.

Still, he had no reason to think it was anything else.

Following Carrie, he went into the shop. The white-haired jeweler looked up from his work. At first the man saw only Carrie, but then his gaze went past the lovely woman and fixed on Slocum.

"You are back, eh? You represent Mr. Barclay?"

"Not today. The lady's got a few rocks for you to look at." Slocum took the stones from Carrie and dropped them on the counter.

"Yes, please see if they are valuable," she said. "I need to know."

Slocum wanted to caution Carrie to remain quiet about the perceived value of the stones, but it was too late. Twice in a week he had come into the same shop and talked to the same jeweler about studying diamonds.

Slocum turned his attention to the jeweler, who went through the same process he had used before. He dropped one stone after another, dividing them into two piles. The jeweler scooped up one group and handed them to Slocum.

"These are worthless, rocks, nothing more. Not even a trace of value. But those, well ..." He rubbed his chin, then looked from Slocum to Carrie and then down again to the four stones he'd kept. "Those are diamonds. Not good ones, mind you, but still diamonds."

"I knew it!" cried Carrie. "John, we—"

"Wait," Slocum said, silencing her. To the jeweler he said, "They're worth something. How much?"

"Oh, not much, not much. I'll give you a good price for them, though."

"How much?" Slocum and Carrie asked in unison.

"A hundred dollars. That's twenty-five dollars each. Generous, very generous."

"That's all?" Carrie's disappointment was obvious.

"Give us back the diamonds," Slocum said. "The gems aren't for sale."

"Wait, John. I need the money. I—"

"They're not for sale," Slocum insisted. He watched the play of emotion on the jeweler's face and knew the diamonds were worth more, a lot more. He'd started to put them into his pocket when the gray-haired jeweler grabbed his wrist.

"I told you before I would find others to join me to buy the other diamonds. I can purchase these with my own funds and do not need their approval."

"A thousand dollars," Slocum said, picking the first number that came to mind. The shock the jeweler showed told him how close he had hit to the target. "For any three of them."

"Out of the question. I can give you five hundred for three."

"For two," Slocum insisted.

"John, this is—" began Carrie. She fell silent when the jeweler agreed. He leafed through a stack of greenbacks and gave Slocum and Carrie the money, then carefully restudied the gems, selecting a pair.

"Talk to your partners," Slocum said as they started to

leave. "We'll be back with more soon enough." The jeweler cackled and stroked his newly purchased diamonds as if they were purring cats.

"I'll be ready," he said. "I assure you, I will be able to buy all you bring if you only give me a few more days!"

"John," Carrie said breathlessly once they were outside. "I can't believe this. He offered nothing for it and you got five hundred dollars."

"Here," Slocum said, handing her the sheaf of bills.

"Wait, you did the work. You deserve a share. Take half."

Slocum ran his fingers over the scrip, considering what a pile of diamonds might bring. Then he considered his position.

"I feel caught in the middle of a gunfight," he told Carrie. "I'm working for Barclay, and now it looks as if I'm working for you too. A man can't serve two masters." His mind raced. Barclay had given him shares in the Great California Land Company, enough to make him filthy rich. And Carrie had shared her bounty with him too.

"Two *masters*?" she teased.

"You know what I mean. It might turn out you and Barclay are working different sides of the road. He's buying land hand over fist, and you got these from some prospectors who just might have picked them up on Barclay's property."

"It's nothing we can't work out, John," she assured him. "Now, I want to find a place to *spend* some of this money. It's been so long since I felt cool linen sheets and a soft mattress." She moved closer. "Shared with a man like you," she added in a sexy whisper.

"Barclay stayed at a hotel just down the street that fits the bill," Slocum said, remembering his earlier thought about being in the Palace Hotel with Carrie Sinclair.

They got a room, no questions asked. San Francisco was

an urbane city, and the Palace Hotel had a reputation for discretion to maintain.

As soon as the door clicked behind them, leaving them alone in the elegant hotel room, Carrie spun about, arms outstretched.

"This is the way to live, John," she cried. "This is the way I *want* to live. And I will. We will," she said. "We are going to be rich. We can travel the world. We can go first-cabin."

"Seems a big jump from a few hundred dollars to that kind of money," Slocum said. He took off his hat and unbuckled his gunbelt. That was all the undressing he had to do. Carrie came over and worked on the rest of his clothes in a furious hurry that aroused him as much as seeing the expanses of her creamy white flesh slowly revealed as she took off her own clothing.

Their lips met and crushed together. Slocum felt the woman's breath coming faster and faster. Her naked breasts pressed into his hairy chest. Her nipples hardened and poked into him, but he did not complain. He reached around her, his hands sliding down her silky back and cupping the twin mounds of her buttocks. He grunted a little as he lifted.

Her legs circled his body; then Carrie locked her ankles behind his back. She wiggled and moved and positioned her hips just right. He sank full-length into her. The sudden intrusion took away his strength. Slocum spun around and sat heavily on the edge of the bed. Carrie got her knees on either side of him, then began moving up and down with torturous slowness.

"You feel so good, John. I love the way you fill me. Your heat gives me—passion!" She began lifting and sinking on his hardness faster and faster. Slocum lay back and reached out, taking the woman's breasts in his hands. He stroked over the milky cones, teased the cherry-red hard nubs, and then let his hands creep behind her again. With a swift move, he rolled over.

"Oh, heaven, wonderful, yes, John," she said with a sigh. Carrie opened her emerald eyes and stared at him, but they were fogged with desire.

He rocked to and fro, his hips moving with sure, deep strokes. Every time he fully entered her, a thrill passed through the woman's body. She quaked and shook and trembled. Then a flush began rising on her white flesh, starting at the tops of her breasts and spreading upward to her throat.

He moved faster, the heat from her interior setting fire to his own loins. Faster and faster he moved, driving deep into her until the tide of lava within his body erupted. As it did, Carrie shrieked out in her unleashed lust. She clawed and grabbed and shoved her hips up off the bed to meet his every stroke. Then she sank back, panting and sweaty and looking content.

"See the difference a mattress under us makes, John?" she asked.

"More comfortable, but not necessary," he said. He showed her what he meant. In the luxurious room they discovered too many ways of pleasure to keep track of.

9

Carrie Sinclair slept, breathing softly, her breasts rising and falling under the cool linen sheets. Slocum slid from the bed and went to the window to stare into the street below. He stretched. They had spent a goodly amount of the money made from the diamond sale the day before, but he didn't think the money had been wasted. He had wondered what it would be like spending the night in this sumptuous hotel with a lovely woman like Carrie Sinclair.

He had found out.

And he liked it. He went to the heap of clothes on the floor where they had been discarded in the rush yesterday. He pawed through the pockets until he found the stock certificate Astin Barclay had given him.

"Ten thousand shares," he murmured, looking from the ornate engraving to the sleeping woman. "Might be able to make a pile of money from this." He didn't like working for Barclay and then running off with Carrie now and again to do her bidding. It seemed to Slocum that he *did* have two masters—and neither was his own conscience.

Part of him said Barclay was wrong, yet evidence continued to pile up that diamonds existed on the site of the old gold mine. Barclay wasn't playing it smart to get ownership of the land. Everything he did seemed a vain blunder, yet he always came out ahead. The old woman—Mrs. Rasmussen—had discovered a rock everyone thought was a diamond. When it turned out that it wasn't, Barclay had been able to purchase vast tracts of land. But he had not bought them at a discount. Instead he had reimbursed the men for what they had paid, and more.

It was almost as if Barclay could afford to be generous because he knew the diamonds were on Emerson's land.

Slocum sighed. That was the problem as he saw it. Barclay didn't own the land most likely to carry the vein of blue dirt cradling the diamonds. Even if he owned everything around it, so what? The mine ought to give the biggest chance of finding more of the diamonds.

And where *had* Barclay gotten his bag of gems? They probably belonged to Emerson—legally, at any rate. Carrie's were similarly suspect, but Slocum wasn't going to hunt down Henry Emerson and point out this breach of law.

He pulled on his jeans and buttoned his shirt. Carrie stirred and tossed her head, a small smile curling her lips. She looked like an angel fallen into his bed. Her bright hair lay in a shining copper halo around her oval face. Slocum could sit and simply stare at her all day, but he was growing restless and didn't know why.

Pulling on his boots, he stood and settled his Colt Navy in its holster. He left quietly, intending to find something to eat. As he walked down the broad stairs into the Palace lobby, he heard a boisterous voice he recognized well. He slowed, then stopped.

Astin Barclay stood just outside the main doors, snapping his fingers and loudly calling for a cab. A carriage rattled up and Barclay said loud enough for Slocum to hear, "Embarcadero, and hurry. The *Cape Fear* will be in on the tide!"

Slocum took the steps down two at a time, and got to

the curb in time to see Barclay's carriage rolling in the direction of the waterfront. He went around the building to the Palace's stables and got his horse. He chafed at the time it took to saddle and mount. He galloped furiously after the carriage, worrying he would miss something important. Why had Barclay come back to San Francisco? The man had been fearful of traveling without a bodyguard before. The reason for making the trip from Oroville had to be all-consuming.

Reining back, Slocum saw Barclay at the end of a dock, hands clasped behind his back. He paced the narrow dock like a caged tiger. Out in the Bay a China clipper had hove to. A longboat made its way slowly toward the dock and Astin Barclay.

Slocum tethered his horse and made his way down to sea level. Carefully picking his way along under the dock, he got almost directly under Barclay by the time the longboat banged into the dock and a dapper man built like a piece of spring steel jumped out. He wore a velvet-tab collared coat, brilliantly polished boots, and a brocade vest festooned with dangling gold chains and society emblems.

"Astin, you shouldn't have come out like this," the man began.

"I wanted to greet you and see if you have the, uh, the package."

"Of course," the man snapped. His British accent seemed oddly out of place along the docks. He was cultured and spoke with clipped precision.

"I need it," said Barclay.

"Don't be absurd. The deal was not for you to take delivery. We will not change anything."

"Almost all the land has been purchased. The Great California Land Company is a great success!" Barclay said with a laugh.

The man with him was not similarly amused. "I expected no less from you."

"You have any quarrel with me, Ian, and—"

"Enough of this," said the Britisher. "I have experienced a harrowing trip and need to recover."

"When will you—"

"When I am ready," came the peevish answer. "A watched pot never boils, you know. Go and stir it more, if you please, sir!"

"Very well, Ian. I just thought I'd be able to help you."

Ian said nothing. Barclay nodded briskly, then set off. At first his walk showed dejection, but as he went on a liveliness came back into it, and Slocum thought the man was actually singing to himself by the time he vanished from sight.

Slocum pulled himself up from under the docks, then froze. He had not been the only one spying on Barclay and his mysterious friend. The old woman from Oroville, Mrs. Rasmussen, stood in a doorway not ten yards away. Slocum waited until she left and made her way into San Francisco before quitting his post. By then, the man named Ian had vanished.

Scratching his head, Slocum walked to the end of the dock and shaded his eyes with his hand. The ship had come around the Cape to judge by its beaten and battered look. He turned and spoke to a sailor tossing a coil of rope into the longboat.

"That the *Cape Fear*?" he asked, pointing to the clipper ship.

"Course she is," the sailor said with contempt. "Just came in, sailin' from up south."

"I was looking for a passenger," Slocum said. He described the man he had seen talking to Barclay. "Ian's his name. British accent. Very well dressed, considering the trip that ship must have had."

"Oh, the limey?" The salt laughed. "He didn't ride with us round the Cape. Joined us not a hundred miles down the coast when we put in for fresh water. Leaky casks we have on the good ship *Fear*."

"He is British, though?"

"Reckon he might be, mister," said the sailor. "Paid well and talked all high and mighty, like he was owner of the ship."

"Might he be?"

"Captain's the owner. Never lets any of the crew forget it neither."

Slocum sat on the edge of the dock, his legs dangling over. The salt dropped beside Slocum and accepted fixings for a cigarette.

"Thank ye mightily," said the sailor, rolling a smoke. "Been a spell since I tasted terbacky. I put on in Georgia for the trip, but the captain's not inclined to let anybody smoke aboard. Fire, he says, sinks a ship faster than a hole in the hull. Don't know about that." The sailor inhaled deeply, held it, then exhaled slowly.

"Did Ian have any diamonds with him?"

"The limey? He was always going on 'bout some company he worked for. DeBeers, it was. Made like he wasn't from England as much as from some other Cape."

"Cape of Good Hope?"

"That's the one. Across the Atlantic from Cape Horn, he said. Something about flowers blooming year round. Don't know about that. And he kept going on about the Orange River and the fabulous wealth to be had there if you was a hardworking, honest bloke. That's his word. Bloke." The sailor silently accepted the fixings for another cigarette, rolled it, and lit the new one from the old. He flipped the butt into the Bay. "You from Georgia too? Recognize the accent."

Slocum had no desire to talk about his family or Slocum's Stand, or even hint at the crime he had committed in killing a carpetbagger judge intent on stealing the spread. He turned the conversation to other paths where he felt more comfortable.

Slocum and the sailor talked idly for another ten minutes, enjoying their smokes. When it became obvious to Slocum he wasn't going to find out any more about the ship's mysterious—and recent—passenger, he got to his feet.

"Smooth sailing back home," Slocum said in parting to the sailor.

"What's your business with him? The limey?"

Slocum shrugged and said, "I'm not sure. Yet." With that, he headed back to the Palace Hotel, wondering what, if anything, he should tell Carrie.

She was just stirring and stretching awake when he returned, and idle talk was the last thing on her mind, which suited Slocum just fine.

10

Slocum didn't feel a bit guilty about taking three days before starting back to Oroville. He was getting accustomed to the terrain along the road, and considered a job with Wells Fargo as a shotgun messenger if he decided to stay in the area much longer. He had spent his time with Carrie feeling alternately ecstatic and depressed, not sure what to do about the stock he owned in Barclay's Great California Land Company or Carrie's obvious greed for finding more diamonds to support a lavish life in San Francisco.

Seldom had Slocum seen people whose greed exceeded their common sense succeed. Greed made men—and women—do stupid things. Out West, stupidity meant death.

Still, if he played his cards right, he wondered if he might not be driven to the Union Club in his own carriage, a lavishly dressed Carrie on his arm, for a night of high-stakes gambling. And it wouldn't matter if he won or lost, because he'd be a diamond magnate. He would have enough money to buy the damned club if he wanted.

"What's wrong, John? You look as if you bit into a lemon," she said as they rode along.

He tried to ease his sour expression, and couldn't. "I was just thinking what it would be like sitting at a poker game and not caring if I won or lost."

"If you had all the money you'd ever need? That's good, John."

"No," he told the redhead, "it's not. I gamble to survive sometimes, but the thrill is in the winning. Outdoing the other players, risking it all. If there was never any risk, there'd be no fun."

"But living hand-to-mouth is not living at all!" she protested. "If you decided not to gamble, you could do anything you wanted. We'll be rich, John. I feel it." It was her turn to look pensive.

He started to ask what else was going through her mind, then was distracted by the wagons rumbling along ahead of them. He had noticed the ruts in the road were deeper than before, but Slocum had not given any thought as to why. Now he knew.

"Land rush again," he said. "What changed?"

"What do you mean?" Carrie studied the wagons, but did not understand what the heaps of goods hidden under tarps meant.

"We left Oroville with Barclay buying up land all over. He had convinced everyone the old woman—Mrs. Rasmussen—had not found a diamond. That let Barclay get back to trying to corner the land. But this has the stench of a land rush."

"No, we dallied too long," she said, but the words lacked any real emotion. It was as if she had gone dry inside. "We need to find the prospectors and get the exact location where they found the diamonds. We can buy that land, or negotiate for it, and—"

"Barclay's in the saddle now, and we'll have to go wherever he tells us," said Slocum. As they rode down Oroville's main street, he saw the booming business conducted by all the merchants. He also saw where Mrs. Rasmussen had her table set up again in the general store. A half-dozen men and women crowded around her. Slocum wondered what the woman had been doing in San Francisco. She might have sparked this new rush of greed to buy the land by telling about Barclay meeting with Ian, the diamond agent from DeBeers.

"Stop, John. I need to talk to them." Carrie dropped from her horse and ran to where two men sat on the boardwalk in front of a saloon, passing a bottle back and forth between them.

Slocum caught at the reins of Carrie's horse, then dismounted and followed her to the saloon. She crouched down and talked urgently with the two. Slocum tried to remember where he had seen them before. Both were familiar, the larger of the pair especially so, but he couldn't put his finger on it. He shrugged. He had seen so many people since coming to Oroville, he couldn't expect to remember them all.

Still . . .

"John, these are the prospectors who found the, uh, the merchandise we took to San Francisco."

"Who's he?" one said. Their nervousness exceeded mere disquiet at being in town and seeing too many people jammed shoulder to shoulder. The way they turned, as if trying to hide from Slocum, sparked his curiosity again. These weren't miners he had seen at the hydraulic mine, or land grabbers intent on staking a claim. And they didn't have the look of prospectors about them either.

"Where'd you gents find the rocks you gave Miss Sinclair?" Slocum asked. The two jumped as if he had stuck them with a needle.

"Got to go."

"Wait, I need to know more—" Carrie said. She looked flustered at the way the pair rushed off, one clinging to the mostly empty bottle and the other making windmill motions with his arms. Both kept looking back over their shoulders as if Slocum might backshoot them.

"Why did you spook them like that, John?"

"I don't recall where I've seen them," Slocum said slowly. He shook his head. "Might be nothing."

"We need to know where they got the diamonds," Carrie insisted.

"They don't know they gave you diamonds, do they?"

She shook her head. "Can't rightly say. Don't think they do, since most of the prospectors hunt for ore with gold and silver in it. Blue clay is different. After all, it had been overlooked all these years by knowledgeable geologists."

"You mean Emerson sent out geologists?"

"I suppose he did," she said. The redhead was as flustered as her two prospectors. "Wouldn't you? I mean, you need to know where the gold is and there's always the chance you might be missing some."

"I can do that. Doesn't take a geologist. Mostly, they cost too much and don't tell you enough," Slocum said. He was beginning to wonder at the swirl of mystery all around him. Too much didn't ring true. Carrie knew things she shouldn't, or was she merely assuming? He had to get off where he could think. And Oroville wasn't likely to provide any peace with new wagon trains rattling into town every few minutes.

If the growth continued like this much longer, Oroville would be ten times the size it had been when the hydraulic mine was running full tilt.

"I've got business to tend to," Slocum told the redhaired woman. He wanted to work out everything with her, but he had to get straight with Astin Barclay first. Slocum knew he would only butt heads if he tried helping Carrie find the source of the diamonds the two prospectors had brought her *and* worked with Barclay corralling all the land around Oroville.

"I need to see to . . . other matters myself," she said, looking distraught. She started to say more to him, then flashed a weak smile, turned, and hurried away in the direction of her boardinghouse. Slocum watched until she turned the corner, then set out to find Barclay.

Halfway down the main street Slocum stopped and stared. A huge banner stretched across the front of a building he remembered as having been abandoned only a week earlier. Slocum had to read the hurriedly painted banner twice before he went over to peer in the front window.

"Don't that beat all," he muttered to himself. Inside the single large room sat the white-haired jeweler he had seen in San Francisco only days before. The man had to have purchased the diamonds from Carrie, closed his shop, and ridden like the wind to get here.

"What's going on in there?" Slocum asked a man lugging a burlap bag of rocks up the rickety steps.

"Buyin' diamonds, that's what. He's a jeweler from San Francisco. Payin' for any we can find."

"Are you finding much?" Slocum had to ask.

"Can't say. I pick up anything I think might be a diamond and bring it in. Some folks, don't know their names, have become millionaires, though."

"He paid them millions?" Slocum asked, staring at the jeweler as he worked his loupe around to peer at a rock Slocum knew to be worthless, even at this distance.

"I, well, don't know. Somebody did. Everybody knows people are gettin' rich findin' diamonds and sellin' them!" The man grunted as he dragged his bag into the store to get into line.

"Always it's a friend's friend who strikes it rich," Slocum said to himself. He wondered if he and Carrie had sparked the jeweler's move from a small shop off Portsmouth Square to this huge storefront in Oroville. Or if something more was at work. The jeweler's association with moneyed men in San Francisco might have solidified enough to allow him to buy—though Slocum saw more examining than buying.

Truth to tell, he watched and didn't see the jeweler buying any diamonds. He decided to check out the operation for a spell.

Slocum settled into a chair and watched the people parading past. No one seemed to be emerging from the jeweler's clutching money from diamond sales, but everyone's spirits were high and all had stories of how others were getting rich.

When he saw Astin Barclay strutting along down the middle of the street, greeting people as he came on like a one-man parade, Slocum levered himself from the chair and stepped into the hot sun.

"Mr. Slocum, you are here again. Where did you go? So much has happened." Barclay had not even said hello.

"Noticed the jeweler we saw in San Francisco has moved here," Slocum said, jerking his thumb in the direction of the shop.

"He smells a fortune to be made. He has worked a deal with influential backers, I am told. He can purchase any diamond found in these hills for whatever it takes—and is doing so."

"How much has he spent for these diamonds?"

"I don't know," Barclay said, frowning. "Your attitude is one of skepticism, my good man. That is entirely uncalled for. My success is going to be legendary soon, I trust."

"You have all the land surrounding the mine bought up?"

"Almost," Barclay said. "I have to fight off others trying to steal away the mineral rights, but I have been there first in most cases and with the best offer. All that remains is to purchase the mine."

"You sound worried about that. Has Emerson turned down your offer?"

"Sir, a word in private." Barclay took Slocum's elbow and steered him from the middle of the street. He waved cordially to many citizens of the town as he maneuvered Slocum to a shady spot in an alley between a bakery and a dry-goods store. The bonhomie vanished when he was out of public view.

"You look worried," Slocum said.

"I am," Barclay confided. "I have spent about all the money I have purchasing land. I haven't enough left for the central purchase, the part that will guarantee our fortune. I need a considerable sum of money to offer Emerson. Otherwise, he will only laugh at me."

"Seeing this frenzy to find diamonds, don't you think he would send his own geologist back to hunt for your vein of diamonds?" Slocum frowned. He didn't even know if that was the proper term. Did diamonds come in veins, like gold and silver?

"This is another reason we must strike while the iron is hot," said Barclay. He chewed at his lower lip. "Emerson has been up the coast and might not have heard of this strike. We need to buy before he can raise the price."

"If you don't have enough to make a decent offer on the mine, what are you going to do? Explore around the area?" Slocum tried to envision the terrain and how this might work for Barclay. He didn't know enough of where Barclay had purchased land for it to mean much.

"I *must* have that land," Barclay insisted. "I am no neophyte. I know where the majority of the diamonds are to be found. But I need money!"

"Can you promise Emerson a share if you take over the mining? Half a loaf is better than none," Slocum pointed out.

"No! This is my big chance to strike it rich. I will not allow it to slip away from me. I want you to find Emerson, travel up and down the coast until you find him, then make an offer. I will come up with the money somehow, if it is not too much. He might not know yet. I count on it.''

''I wouldn't get my hopes puffed up too much if I were you,'' Slocum said. A new caravan rumbled into town. A half-dozen men rode guard for the luxurious carriage in which two men sat in comfort. Slocum guessed the well-dressed man with the black silk top hat and leaning on a gold-headed cane was Emerson. He recognized immediately the man riding beside the mine owner.

The diamond agent from DeBeers and Emerson exchanged comments and laughed as if they had the world by the tail.

11

Slocum paced behind the stables, thinking hard. He ought to get on his horse and ride. It didn't matter where. Things in Oroville had gotten too complicated for him to figure out. He wasn't even sure what side he wanted to be on.

Astin Barclay had paid him decently to act as bodyguard, but since the land rush had begun, he hadn't needed protection—or so it seemed. If he ever had. Something about the road agents the first time he and Barclay had gone to San Francisco bothered Slocum. The robbery attempt had been too inept. Even a greenhorn could have staged a better robbery. But there was something more about it that still tugged at the corners of Slocum's mind.

He simply couldn't put it into words.

Barclay didn't seem to mind how much time Slocum spent with Carrie either. She bustled about, trying to line up men to work for her, to get deeds to land Barclay had missed, doing every little thing that would open the funnel and pour diamonds into her lap. Even the two prospectors who had given her the four diamonds were busy running her errands.

Worst of all was the torrential flood of men from San Francisco. The jeweler had come to Oroville to make a fortune. Slocum couldn't figure if the man had bought even a single diamond, yet he continued to ask any and all to bring him their rocks in case they happened upon a decent stone. Rumors held that the white-haired man had bought millions of dollars worth of stones. As far as Slocum could tell, these were only rumors.

Then there was the DeBeers agent and Emerson, come to town in the midst of diamond fever. Barclay would never get Emerson to sell, no matter the price. The man owned the hottest property around, and had the financial backing to exploit a new kind of mining. The DeBeers agent, Ian Cuegant by name, had the expertise to open a mine for Emerson. Why sell to Barclay at any price when a new fortune beckoned?

Slocum saw nothing to keep him in Oroville—except Carrie Sinclair. He came to a decision. He threw his saddle on his horse and prepared to ride out to the redhead's boardinghouse and ask her to leave town with him.

"John!"

He turned to see her silhouetted in the stable doorway. For a moment, the sunlight caught her red hair and turned it into spun gold. Then she stepped forward and turned into just another shadow inside the livery.

"I was coming to see you," Slocum said.

"Good, John. Have you heard the news?"

"What news?" He didn't want to stand around gossiping. If they rode hard, they could get to the coast in a day or two and head north. He still had the notion of raising Appaloosas, at least for the summer.

"Barclay is trying to raise enough money to buy the mine from Emerson. He is selling shares in his company and—"

"The Great California Land Company?"

"Yes, that's the one. He is using the land he already

owns as collateral to raise even more. With the money he can convince Emerson to sell.''

''Nonsense,'' said Slocum. ''Why would Emerson bring in Ian Cuegant if he didn't intend to reopen his mine, this time looking for diamonds?''

''Barclay is sure he can buy him off.''

''He tried to stop Cuegant from even coming here,'' Slocum said. He saw Carrie's face go pasty white. ''I saw them on the dock in San Francisco. Barclay and Cuegant know each other. I didn't hear much, but it sounded as if Barclay was trying to convince Cuegant to either turn around and go home or maybe work for him. He had to know Emerson was bringing in an expert to mine the diamonds.''

The shock left Carrie's face. She put a hand to her throat and let out a breath she had been holding. ''I thought it was something else,'' Carrie said.

''I also saw Mrs. Rasmussen at the dock. I think she triggered the buying here when she saw Barclay and Cuegant together. She must have thought Barclay was selling her a bill of goods about the diamond she supposedly found in the turkey craw.''

''She *knew* diamonds were around?'' asked Carrie, still breathless.

''From all I've heard, she got together with the owner of the general goods store and a few others trying to buy land. Barclay had a jump on her—and Emerson is holding all the trumps.''

''Barclay isn't saying, but he must believe the majority of the diamonds are on the old mine site,'' said Carrie.

''That's the way I see it. There's nothing I can do to make a dime. I wanted you to . . .'' Slocum bit off his invitation for her to join him on the ride north when he saw Astin Barclay just outside the stable. The man hurried along as was his wont but behind him trailed two men—wearing their bandannas as masks.

"Stay here," he said suddenly, his hand going for his Colt Navy. He pushed past the startled woman and burst into the bright sunlight. Turning left, he didn't see either Barclay or the men trailing him. He dashed down the alley and burst out into the open field immediately behind the livery stable. Barclay had his hands in the air, the two men backing him away from town, their six-shooters drawn.

"Mr. Slocum!" called Barclay, seeing him. "Help!"

Slocum cursed. If Barclay had held his tongue, the two men would have filled new graves in the potter's field at the other end of town. Both swung around, six-guns blazing. Slocum dived and hit the ground hard. He rolled and came up behind the remnants of a wagon. Wood splinters flew in all directions as the outlaws' slugs ripped through the rotted wood.

Seeing that the wagon provided scant protection, Slocum kept moving. He rose from behind a low pile of firewood and snapped off two quick shots. Both missed. Slocum crouched and tried to make it to a stump. A bullet caught his heel and sent him tumbling.

He hit the ground hard, rolled, and kept rolling as dirt flew up all around from the outlaws' bullets. Barclay was screaming something he couldn't understand. Mostly, Slocum didn't know why the man stood by stupidly instead of running for cover.

Slocum came up to his knees behind the stump, rested the butt of his six-shooter on the stump, and squeezed off an accurate shot that spun one outlaw around. It wasn't a killing shot; it had only winged him. Still, it evened the odds a mite.

"Barclay, run for it!" Slocum shouted. He fired twice more at the outlaw still standing in the middle of the field not ten feet from Barclay. "Drop down!" Slocum fired his last round and had to work to reload.

He kept glancing out, seeing that Barclay stood as still

as a statue. This lent haste to his reloading. If the outlaw turned his pistol from Slocum to Barclay, it would be an easy kill.

"Hey!" shouted Slocum, trying to draw the outlaw's attention—and fire. He squeezed off another round, only to find he again faced two gunmen. The one he had wounded sat up, clutching his side, but this small wound didn't stop him from shooting.

Slocum gathered his feet under him, knowing he had to make a full frontal assault. If he charged, he might take the pair by surprise. He couldn't tell, but thought they were the same two who had tried to bushwhack them on the road. If so, they were likely to cut and run rather than fight.

As he charged them, Slocum caught sight of Carrie Sinclair from out of the corner of his eye.

"Carrie, get back, watch out!" he shouted. The woman came on, as if she didn't know what was going on. Slocum dug his heels into the soft dirt, changed directions, and headed for her as the two outlaws turned their guns in her direction. He fired repeatedly to drive them back.

Then he smashed headlong into the woman, sending her flying. Slocum lost his balance and went down. Hot lead seared its way across his back as he fell. He had missed being killed by fractions of an inch. He landed flat on his belly. A large rock in the middle of his chest knocked the wind from his lungs. Gasping like a fish out of water, he struggled to focus his eyes, to get his Colt turned in the outlaws' direction, to fire, to simply stay alive.

He sucked hard, and all he got into his lungs was liquid fire that blurred his vision.

"John?" he heard from a thousand miles away. "John!"

He blinked hard and saw Carrie kneeling above him.

"Get down," he grated out. "They're trying to kidnap Barclay. Don't let them shoot you." He reached out, weak as a kitten. The six-gun fell from his grip as the shakes hit him. Then he regained a measure of control over his body as breath gusted back into his lungs. He rolled onto his side and picked up the fallen six-shooter.

But there was nothing to fire at. The two outlaws—and Astin Barclay—were gone.

"What's going on, John? I heard the shots, I saw you, everything is so muddled!"

He sat up, ignoring the pain in his chest. Twisting slightly gave him a new source of agony. The lead slug had barely missed robbing him of life. Instead, it left behind a legacy of torment for a foot or more on his back.

"Barclay. Did they take him?" Slocum managed.

"He was kidnapped? I didn't know what was going on."

"I know them. The men who took Barclay," Slocum said. He fixed his green eyes squarely on the lovely redhead's pale face when he said, "So do you."

"What? What are you saying?"

"You know the men who kidnapped him."

"I—they—the two out here? Why, yes, I do. But they couldn't have *kidnapped* Barclay."

"They were the pair of prospectors you got the diamonds from, weren't they?"

"Yes, that's why I am so confused about this. You say they kidnapped Mr. Barclay? Why? They're prospectors, not criminals."

"They're road agents," Slocum said, angry at himself for not having recognized them earlier. Their actions when Carrie had spoken to them ought to have alerted him. Still, he had not gotten a good look at them before. But the pain and getting the wind knocked out of him had knocked some sense into him. Slocum thought the larger of the two road agents might have been the man who bushwhacked him at the Gold Trident. Now that he knew them, he could track them down.

He stood, then went dizzy from pain. Carrie caught him,

her arm supporting his weight as he staggered.

"You need a doctor, John," she said.

"I need to get after them. They took Barclay."

"It's not your job. We'll let the marshal know, and he can get a posse or something."

Slocum snorted derisively. He had seen the town marshal. The man might be good at busting up fights between drunken miners, but his expertise ended there. The marshal didn't have the hardness it took to actually track down an outlaw.

"It *is* my job," Slocum said. "Barclay hired me to protect him. I didn't do a very good job."

"Your pride's wounded," she countered. "You feel responsible and want to rescue him to make it right. Let the law handle this. We need to get you to a doctor."

Every move sent white-hot lances into him, making breathing difficult again. He worried a rib might have been cracked by the bullet.

"Let's get this over with," Slocum said, seething at the need for a doctor—and the time it would take. He wanted to be on the trail before it got cold.

He was wrapped up like a mummy. Slocum stretched and endured the jab of pain as he moved.

"Don't go aggravatin' that now, son," said the doctor. "You need to get some bed rest."

"I'll see that he gets it, Doctor," said Carrie, a smile on her lips and a wicked gleam in her eye.

"Rest," the doctor insisted. "Any wrestlin' match is likely to open up that wound. It's not serious, but surely does hurt like a whole hill of ants moved in, don't it, son?"

"Yeah," Slocum agreed, getting into his shirt. The long, bloody rip in the fabric looked worse than the shallow trough in his hide. He stood, let the lightheadedness pass, then motioned to Carrie to leave.

"Here, Doctor. Thank you," she said, paying. Slocum started to protest, then bit back his words. She had been the reason Barclay's kidnappers had gotten away. If she hadn't wandered like an innocent into the middle of a gunfight, he would never have been shot.

"Let's go tell the marshal," she said.

Slocum shook his head. "I don't think there's any call for that. Reckon he already knows."

They walked down the street to the jailhouse. The marshal and a deputy stood outside, arguing. A crowd had formed around them

"There's no need to go after him, Claude. I tell you, wait for the ransom. It's gonna come, you mark my words," said the deputy. The marshal wasn't taking much to convince him.

"No posse, men," the marshal called out. Sweat beaded his forehead.

The three men standing near Slocum got into an argument. One pushed the other two away and said, "I ain't sellin'! I bought them shares of Great California Land Company fair and square."

"We'll give you double what you paid for them," one of the other two said.

"Wait, wait," said Slocum, stepping between the men. "Why are you bidding up the stock like this? The owner's been kidnapped. They might even kill him if there's nobody to pay their ransom."

"You see any heirs? Mr. Barclay's shares will be tore up and forgotten. That leaves a bigger cut of the pie for the rest of us!"

The ripple of greed passed through the crowd. Soon, a half-dozen men were actively buying and selling shares of Barclay's Great California Land Company. Slocum shook his head in amazement.

The bottom ought to have dropped out of the stock price when everyone learned the head of the company was kidnapped and might even be dead. Instead, it set off a buying frenzy that made earlier hysteria look calm in comparison.

12

"I shot it out with the two that kidnapped Barclay," Slocum told the marshal. The man's face went pale under his weathered skin at the mention of the gunfight. He opened his mouth, moved it around like a beached fish gasping for breath, then clamped it shut.

"I can't leave town," he finally said. "Not with things poppin' and sizzlin' in hot grease the way they are here."

"A man was spirited away under your nose," Slocum told him. "I winged one of the kidnappers. You and a couple deputies can get him back before they've gone another ten miles."

"I'd need a posse, and that's not gonna happen," the marshal said, getting back some of his color as he thought of ways around going after Astin Barclay. "A dozen of them saw the kidnapping and did nothing about it. You were the only one—and why not? He's payin' you a fat salary to be his bodyguard. I don't get but thirty dollars a month, plus any process I happen to serve. Ain't much of that to do either, not with the Gold Trident closing like it did." He cleared his throat and hitched up his gunbelt as if coming to a decision. "I need to ask around and see if anyone knows who done it."

114

"Why? What difference does it make knowing who kidnapped Barclay? He's in danger of being killed. Does it matter who pulls the trigger if you can save him before the bullet leaves the barrel?"

"I don't want to go rushin' into anything, mister. I need to be sure of myself before I risk anyone's life."

Slocum turned to Carrie and sneered. "I told you it'd be this way." He had let her goad him into demanding the marshal do something. Slocum had known it would turn out this way. The marshal didn't have a backbone. He could spend the rest of his life interrogating the fine citizens of Oroville about what they had seen and never get around to putting his butt onto saddle leather and riding out to save Barclay.

"But John, he can't do this!" she protested loudly. "He's the marshal!"

Slocum took her arm and steered her down the street. He felt antsy about going after Barclay. The man was in jeopardy, and Slocum had agreed to be his bodyguard. The failure out in the field where Barclay had been kidnapped made Slocum struggle to put his finger on what was not right.

"Others watched him being hauled off," Slocum said suddenly. "The marshal said so."

"What do you mean?" asked Carrie. The woman tossed her hair around like a red whip. It caught lightly in the brisk hot wind blowing down the street. A look of worry vanished as her hair blew back and momentarily hid her face.

"If you want to kidnap someone, why do it in front of a dozen witnesses?" Slocum knew the pair were the same ones as the road agents. They had been inept at every illegal pursuit they tried, except maybe the damage at the Gold Trident. The bigger of the pair had bushwhacked Slocum neat enough then. The only thing that had ever got them any real money had to be selling Carrie the diamonds they'd found. Or had they really just happened on them? The pair didn't look much like prospectors to Slocum. "You know them," he went on. "Did they seem like sharp men?"

"Smart? Hardly. What does it take to be a prospector other than a desire to be alone a lot?"

"Don't often see prospectors working in teams. They're solitary folks. Two or three might work a claim, but miners are a different breed from prospectors."

"I don't know what you're getting at. Are you accusing me of something? Like being in cahoots with them?"

"What would it gain you to have Barclay kidnapped?" Slocum said. He shook his head and stared straight ahead. Her question had taken him by surprise.

"Nothing," she said too quickly. "I want to buy the mine from Emerson and keep it from Barclay, but only because of the incredible money to be made. I don't even know Barclay."

Slocum let that lie pass. He had seen them arguing outside the land office. "I've got to get on their trail pronto," he said. With one being wounded like he is, they won't ride too far too fast. I should overtake them before sundown." Slocum judged the position of the sun in the sky and knew it would be easy to track the trio in broad daylight.

One was wounded, and Barclay probably didn't ride too well. More than that, the two owlhoots were bumbling fools. This worried Slocum as much as anything. He had the feeling the kidnapping had been staged, but for whose pleasure? And for what reason? Many in the town had watched and done nothing. The marshal wasn't likely to poke his nose outside his jailhouse until he knew it was safe. Oroville wasn't the kind of town where people got involved in each other's problems.

"Emerson," Carrie said suddenly. "That has to be it.

Emerson is responsible for the kidnapping.''

"Why?"

"He, uh, he doesn't want to sell the mine, and knows Mr. Barclay wants it badly.''

"Emerson is a businessman. If Barclay offered enough he'd sell it in the wink of an eye. It ought to be the other way around. Emerson might get abducted by Barclay because he wouldn't want to sell the mine.''

"Oh," Carrie said in a small voice. "I suppose you are right, John. This is all so frightening!''

"Get on back to the boardinghouse and wait for me there. I'll be back before you know I'm gone.''

She smiled wickedly and said, "I doubt that." She impetuously kissed him, then hurried off. Slocum didn't know what to make of any of this. The robbery on the way to San Francisco had been a botch. He saw no good reason for the kidnapping to have succeeded other than blind luck on the part of the outlaws. If Carrie hadn't wandered into the middle of the gunfight, Slocum would have laid both of the men out as customers for the Oroville undertaker.

Mounting, Slocum rode slowly to the field where they had shot it out. A blind man could have followed the obvious tracks. Three had mounted and taken off, not galloping as he'd expected, but trotting. The fleeing trio's gait slowed within a mile to a walk. Slocum began having to work to stay on the scent when they hit a rocky patch.

"Heading for the hydraulic mine?" He looked up the road and thought that a likely destination. The buildings might afford a decent hiding place. No one was likely to wander back there. Certainly none of the miners would. Most had already moved on, hunting for new jobs.

Slocum considered riding around and approaching the mine from the far side. He had the two clumsy crooks cut off right away, if they were at the mine. The deep gorge prevented any hope of them escaping in that direction. If

Slocum had even one more man with him, they could have boxed in the kidnappers easily.

"You might as well climb a tree and then drop pine cones on the head of anyone trailing you," Slocum said aloud. He was one against the pair of them, but he saw how easily they could be cornered if they had sought refuge at the mine.

Less than a mile from the mine's main buildings, Slocum saw fresh horse dung. A muddy patch gave him clear evidence of recent riders going up the road. They had not even tried to hide their tracks. He rode into a stand of pinyon and tethered his horse. He made sure his Colt Navy was loaded, then pulled his Winchester from its saddle sheath.

He checked the rifle carefully, made sure the magazine was full, then set out on foot. Slocum had told Carrie he'd have Barclay back before sundown. He might return to Oroville in less than two hours. As he got closer to the tight knot of deserted buildings at the mine, he slowed his determined pace and sought a vantage point to study the lay of the land.

Slocum had thought he could blunder on into camp and simply take Barclay back. He was glad he had not been so foolish—or careless. He saw two men arguing outside the foreman's shack. One he recognized. The man held his arm to his side as if it hurt like hell and his jeans were soaked with blood. Slocum reckoned he might have hit the man twice during their gunfight. But the other man stood in deep shadow and was obviously not the outlaw's partner in crime.

Working his way closer, Slocum tried to overhear the argument. All he got were tones, not the words themselves. It was apparent from the way the wounded outlaw stood and occasionally dropped his eyes that he was getting reprimanded.

Slocum skirted the shack and went to the stables. He

glanced inside and saw five horses. Two he recognized as belonging to the outlaws he had faced before. The other animals were better groomed and well fed, and the saddles were expensive. Slipping into the stable, he approached the horses slowly, letting them get used to his presence. It wouldn't do if they got spooked and brought unwanted attention down on him.

A few quick saws with a knife almost cut the cinch on the first horse. He had started working on the second when he heard men approaching. Again the men argued.

"Little wonder," Slocum decided. "Those two befoul everything they touch."

Slocum dropped into a crouch and scurried out of the stable. He circled the building in time to see the second of the men enter. It was the uninjured kidnapper. The other man, the one already inside the stable, complained bitterly. The cadence of his talk was strange, but again Slocum could not make out words.

Knowing where two of the men were gave him some hope of getting Barclay out of the camp without too much gunplay. He hurried to the foreman's cabin, pressed his shoulder against the wall, and winced. He moved slower than usual because of the bullet crease he'd received during the earlier shootout. This firmed his resolve to get back Barclay and bring a measure of justice, if not mercy, to the kidnappers.

"Hey, you! It's him. The son of a bitch what shot me!" came the loud cry behind Slocum. He glanced over his shoulder and saw the wounded owlhoot limping into sight. The man lifted a sawed-off shotgun and cut loose with both barrels.

Slocum reacted without thinking, falling flat on his belly. He winced as hot buckshot ripped through the wood just above his head. The report from the scattergun momentarily deafened him so he couldn't hear what the man was shouting now. Turning onto his side, Slocum lifted his six-shooter and got off a shot that sent the man limping for cover.

Then all hell broke loose. Slocum had lead raining down on him from all directions. From inside the foreman's shack came round after round of lead blowing apart the wall until it looked like a piece of Spanish moss hanging down.

Slocum chanced a quick look inside, and saw Barclay sitting in a chair at the far side of the room. He didn't seem to be tied, but he seemed stunned.

"Run!" Slocum shouted at him. "Get the hell out of there, Barclay!"

Slocum snapped a couple more shots at the man with the shotgun to keep him guessing. Slocum got his feet under him, then bulled his way through the demolished wall. He crashed to the dirt floor in time to see the back of a man vanishing out the single door. He shot, causing the man to jerk to the side and curse, then hurry on.

"Barclay!"

"Oh, it's you, Mr. Slocum. You're rescuing me." Barclay sounded surprised at the sudden salvation. He stood and brushed off his clothing. "I should have known you were on the job. You are a diligent man."

"To hell with that. Who are the others?"

"Others? I don't understand."

A new round of gunfire tore through what was left of the cabin. Slocum shoved Barclay back into the only corner of the shack left standing intact. He swung around and fired back in the direction of the stable. He saw not only the scattergun, but a small silvery pistol pointed in his direction. Slocum turned his fire to the hand holding the smaller pistol.

A splinter from the wood hit the gunman's hand, making him drop his pistol.

"Bloody 'ell!" came a loud outcry.

Slocum blinked. British. The man he had disarmed was British.

"We've got to hightail it," Slocum said. "How many of them are there gunning for us? I counted four."

"Four?" Barclay shook off the question. "Yes, I rather suspect there were that many. I did not bother counting."

Slocum began to tell Barclay what he thought of such carelessness when a flash of gold caught his eye. In the doorway of the cabin lay a tiny gold stickpin. Slocum picked it up and thrust it into his pocket, then found himself dodging more lead. The men who had fled through the door had found positions to potshot him.

"We're in a cross fire," Slocum said, ducking back to the dubious shelter of what remained standing of the foreman's shack. "They'll ventilate us if we don't get out of here fast."

"How do you suggest doing it, Mr. Slocum?"

For a man who had been kidnapped, Barclay was well possessed of his senses now. He had been too frightened to count his kidnappers, but now, with bullets ripping through the wood walls and inching toward their heads and hearts, Barclay might have been sitting down at the dinner table for all the alarm he showed.

Slocum turned over the foreman's bed and crouched behind it, reloading. As he worked on his six-gun his mind raced. He doubted the kidnappers had much in the way of ammo. They had not expected a rescue this soon—or ever.

"How much were they asking for you?" he asked Barclay.

"Asking? As ransom? Why, I cannot say. A considerable amount, I should think," said Barclay self-importantly. "I will be an obscenely rich man when I convince Emerson to sell this mine."

"At least you recognize where they took you," Slocum said sarcastically. He glanced up, got the lay of the land in mind, then told Barclay, "When I open fire, you run to the right. Smash on through the wall. It's not going to stand much longer."

"Where do I go then?"

"Head for the bunkhouse but don't go in. It's a door in the side of the hill. I'll be along right on your heels."

"Why—"

Barclay never got a chance to speak. Slocum shoved him hard, started shooting, and then trotted after a stumbling Astin Barclay. Firing methodically kept the kidnappers pinned down.

"Open the door but don't go in," Slocum ordered. Barclay hesitated. Slocum grabbed Barclay's arm and pulled him along to the side of the hill where the bunkhouse was half buried. They tumbled into a pile, protected from view by the bunkhouse. Slocum took the chance to reload. He was out of ammunition now, so six rounds had to get them both out of the jam.

"What are you planning?" asked Barclay.

"Hush." Slocum edged back in time to see a man vanish into the bunkhouse. Then Slocum kicked the door shut, spun around, and fired twice, both rounds striking the man he had wounded before in the chest. The man's arms flew outward, and he dropped the sawed-off shotgun. From the way he gasped, he wasn't long for this world.

Slocum snatched up the shotgun and discharged it in the direction of the other two gunmen. The sudden assault from a shotgun drove both of them to cover. Slocum saw no hint of movement.

He ripped open the fallen man's shirt pocket and got out two more shotgun shells. A quick snap ejected the spent shells, and he dropped in two more. He fired into the bunkhouse door just as the man inside screwed up his courage to come rushing out.

"Slocum, my God! You're killing them!"

"Of course I am," Slocum said. He threw down the empty shotgun. He didn't much care if he had turned the man in the bunkhouse to bloody ribbons or if the man had simply retreated to make a stand. Either way gave Slocum time to get Barclay out of danger.

He hustled the portly man down the hill. They circled and came up the road to where Slocum had tethered his horse.

"Get on behind me," Slocum said, mounting. The horse protested the double weight, but gamely trotted down the road toward Oroville.

"You are my savior, Mr. Slocum. There's only one way I can ever thank you for so gallantly saving my very life."

"What might that be?" asked Slocum.

"I am rewarding you with another five thousand shares of my Great California Land Company!"

Somehow, Slocum wasn't overwhelmed.

13

"A noble rescue. Never have I seen such heroism! Mr. Slocum is a champion like the knights of yore!"

"What's a knight?" one miner hoarsely whispered to another. His companion shrugged and scratched himself as a nit enjoyed a succulent meal at the expense of his crotch. "Must be something special," the first miner went on.

Slocum tried not to look too disgusted at all Astin Barclay was saying. He wanted to get the hell out of the saloon where Barclay had set up shop, but he couldn't do it. Not yet. Barclay had paid him well so far, and he felt he owed the man something, though exactly why he couldn't say. Everything the man had done had spelled nothing but trouble for Slocum, be it kidnapping or highwaymen or trying to keep the crowds mobbing Barclay from tearing him apart, more from eagerness than any malice.

"I have rewarded Mr. Slocum handsomely for his gallantry. I have given him five thousand shares of stock in the Great California Land Company." Barclay gestured grandly and urged Slocum to hold up the elaborate stock certificate with his name written in as owner.

"That much? Why, Benjie Lorgan just bought a hundred shares for a dollar each," gasped another man in the throng.

He knocked back a stiff drink, compliments of Barclay as part of his celebration.

The man's comment brought Slocum up. A dollar a share? He had fifteen thousand shares given him in the Great California Land Company. That made him fabulously rich. If he played his cards right, he might cash in on the frenzy of speculation that seized everyone in Oroville. Slocum didn't know for certain, but he reckoned he might get twice as much as a dollar per share.

More, if he held onto the shares for a spell while the others frothed at the mouth for their piece of the action.

He shook himself to clear the cobwebs dangling over his good sense. All Barclay had given him were two pieces of paper. Worthless paper unless Barclay got Emerson's mine—and unless there were diamonds under the shuttered gold mine. That was a supposition or two more than was likely to pan out. Slocum thought his chances were about the same as drawing to an inside straight.

He stepped back and let Barclay whip the crowd into a frenzy with more free liquor and promises of fantastic returns if they bought into his land company. More money changed hands than Slocum thought existed in the world. Barclay paid fabulous amounts for the rotgut he served. More, far more, went the other direction across the table and into Barclay's deep pockets.

Then Barclay laid down the bomb that caused a deadly silence to fall in the smoky, cramped saloon. Slocum reached for his Colt Navy, though he didn't draw. Yet.

"It's all worthless," Barclay said in a level voice.

"Whatdya mean, worthless?" demanded a man holding five hundred shares of stock he had bartered for his land near the mine. "You lyin' to us?"

"Not at all, my good sir," Barclay said smoothly. "I need, I repeat, I *need* to buy the mine from Mr. Emerson. Without it, all the land already purchased by the Great California Land Company might be as dross. I am sure the majority of the diamonds are to be found on Emerson's property—at the site of the old hydraulic mine.''

"Well, then, we *are* rich," the man shouted.

"Wait, gents, please. Hear me out. I don't have enough money to buy the mine. Emerson is driving a hard bargain."

This made Slocum stiffen and turn his attention from the crowd to Barclay. When had Barclay spoken with the elusive Mr. Emerson? They had missed him in San Francisco. Had they spoken after Emerson and Ian Cuegant arrived in Oroville?

Cuegant. The DeBeers agent. The man with the British accent Barclay had spoken to on the San Francisco docks. He thought the rhythm of speech of the unseen kidnapper out at the mine had been British. That was too much of a coincidence for Slocum to swallow.

Something was going on, and he felt like he was caught in the middle of a tornado, being spun this way and that. And Astin Barclay was mixed up in it all the way to his double chins.

"What are you sayin', Barclay?" demanded a half-dozen men at the same time. "Spit it out."

"I need capital. Money. Greenbacks. Specie. Gold dust. I need it to buy the land that will make us all rich."

"You askin' us for a loan?" The miner laughed. Two others, both merchants Slocum recognized, put their heads together. From the serious expressions on their faces, he knew they were discussing what Barclay said—and they didn't much like it either.

"Not at all. I will *not* go into debt to buy this mine. Rather, I need to sell a few more shares of stock in my land company. The more you buy, the more you'll profit after mining begins. Think of it. Think of being rich. What would you do with the money? You, good sir. What are your dreams?''

Barclay had singled out a smallish man, a drifter from the look of his clothing. The man smiled as if he pictured the most beautiful woman in the world agreeing to spend the night with him.

''I'd settle down, get me some farmland, and get a wife.''

''Hell, man, with the kind of money you can make, you can send off for a dozen mail-order brides!''

Everyone laughed. The man blushed under his leathery tan and said, ''I'm no Mormon. One woman is enough for me!''

This brought more laughter.

Barclay said, ''Even if you are a disciple of the good Brigham Young and want a dozen wives, you'll be able to support them. All your women could live as queens, be they a score or just that one special lady. Lavish them with gifts, and they will lavish their charms on you!''

A cheer went up, and men crowded to give even more money in exchange for the stock certificates. Slocum had seen such rampaging greed before and knew how Barclay played on it. Don't dwell on the risk of hunting for the diamonds—which might not be there. Telling the men how much they would make and getting them mentally spending the money took their minds off practical matters.

Were there any men in the area who knew how to mine diamonds? Slocum didn't know if it required special skill, but he reckoned it might. Diamonds weren't gold.

The tumult in the saloon grew. Slocum tucked away his stock certificate and slipped from the saloon. Astin Barclay was as safe as if he was held in his mama's arms. No man in that saloon would allow any harm to come to the man who would make them all millionaires.

The cold night air erased the heavy sweat on Slocum's

face. As he stepped into the frigid wind, a chill ran up and down his spine. Oroville had lived by the hydraulic mine and was dying when it left. Now it was as robust a town as any boomtown Slocum had ever seen. Merchants arrived daily to sell their goods. Those who had been there for years did a business they hadn't seen since the Gold Trident opened. If anything, they saw Barclay and his diamond company as a salvation. Emerson had doomed them when he closed the mine.

Slocum had to admit Carrie Sinclair had done much to push the owner in that direction. The lovely woman had agitated well and publicly against the destruction wrought by the powerful water cannon chewing away the land and washing it toward the distant Pacific Ocean. She had mustered enough support to force Emerson to close a mine that was becoming less and less profitable.

For all her agitation, Carrie wasn't entirely responsible. The mine would still be operational if Emerson had decided it was worth bringing in lawyers to fight Carrie—or worse. Slocum knew mine owners handled labor problems with hired guns and thugs more comfortable swinging an ax handle at a head than a pick at an ore vein. It wasn't beyond comprehension that Emerson would handle a single woman in the same bloody-handed manner.

Slocum saw few people on the street. Most of the men had crowded inside to get Barclay's free liquor and buy even more shares in the Great California Land Company so the man could buy Emerson's closed mine. But a solitary man striding along with purpose caught Slocum's eye.

Ian Cuegant.

Slocum started to call out, then bit back the outcry. He checked his six-shooter to make sure it rode easy on his hip and came out smoothly into his strong hand. Then Slocum went hunting. For the DeBeers man.

Cuegant ducked down an alley and vanished for a moment, but Slocum headed him off. Running down the main street, Slocum got to the next alley between a bookstore and a Chinese laundry in time to see Cuegant. The DeBeers agent stopped in plain sight, then beckoned to someone out of Slocum's field of vision.

Curious as to whom the man met in the shadows of Oroville, Slocum crept down the alley on cat's feet until he was within a few feet of Cuegant. The DeBeers agent never heard him.

Neither did Carrie Sinclair.

"You are making an incredible mess of this," Carrie said angrily. "How could it all come to this?"

"I did what I was told," Cuegant said, his voice thick with British accent. "When we . . ." Cuegant stopped talking. Slocum knew he had been found out. How did not matter. Maybe Cuegant had the same sixth sense Slocum used to stay alive. Or maybe he was simply downwind.

Cuegant turned, his hand going to a vest pocket. He pulled out a pearl-handled derringer that looked to be the twin to the one lost back in the mine shootout.

Slocum stepped out, knowing time for furtiveness had passed. "Evening, Miss Sinclair," he said, touching the brim of his dusty Stetson. As he spoke, he kept his eyes fixed on Cuegant and the small-frame, large-bore pistol pointed unwaveringly at his chest. "And good evening to you too, Mr. Cuegant."

The man's eyes widened. "Do I know you?"

"Of course you do," Slocum said. "You shot at me out at the mine while I was rescuing Astin Barclay."

"That's outrageous, John. You can't think Mr. Cuegant is involved!" Carrie sounded outraged, but Slocum wondered at her real emotion. She struggled to find the right face to put on. Her words reflected shock; her face showed consternation at having to think up a new lie.

"I know he is. I saw him talking to Barclay on the San Francisco dock. So did Mrs. Rasmussen."

"Who?"

"Mrs. Rasmussen, the woman who found the diamond in her turkey crop," Slocum said. "Or so she said. Turned out to be a fake diamond. Just plain old worthless rock."

Cuegant's aim shifted slightly as he turned toward Carrie as if she could explain all this. Slocum moved faster than a striking rattler. He batted away the derringer with his left hand and clutched Cuegant's throat with the other. Lifting slightly brought the DeBeers agent to his toes and removed all threat.

"John, put him down. There's no need for violence."

"He kidnapped Barclay—or was in on it. Isn't that so, Cuegant?"

"Yes," the man grated out. His fists banged impotently against Slocum's powerful arm, trying to force him to release the grip on his throat. Slocum heaved and sent the man staggering. To prevent any further foolishness, Slocum picked up the derringer and tucked it into his own pocket.

"I don't understand, John. What's going on?" asked Carrie.

He glared at the redhead, then said, "You tell me. What are you and Cuegant doing, getting together out here where nobody can see you?"

"I—we—he—we're not—"

"She approached me to work with her to corner the market on the diamonds, just as my syndicate has done worldwide. DeBeers is interested in any new find, of course."

"Of course," Slocum said dryly. "You and Carrie kidnapped Barclay?"

"No!" came the instant protest from the red-haired woman. "I had nothing to do with it. I—"

"She came to me after that debacle," Cuegant said, smoothing his coat and rubbing his neck where Slocum's fingers had left ugly red marks. "If we work together, may-hap we can get some of the gravy away from Barclay."

"Why'd you kidnap him?" asked Slocum.

"I'd hoped to reason with him, but that didn't work. He's too intent on making a fortune off the diamond find," said Cuegant. "So I had him kidnapped, thinking this would frighten him into seeing things my way."

"You work for Emerson?" asked Slocum. "The pair of you rode into Oroville together?"

"I don't know what's going on, John. Are you saying Mr. Cuegant *works* for Emerson?"

"Can't rightly say who he is working for, except maybe himself." That Slocum understood. All the double-dealing and sneaking around were irritating for him. If a man wanted something, he ought to go for it out in the open for everyone to see, not creep about like some banker or lawyer looking for an underhanded way of doing the same thing.

"I wanted him to lower the selling price on his stock. I'd buy into the company," Cuegant declared. He had finally regained his composure, and Slocum knew he couldn't believe a word that came from those foreign lips now.

"Heard tell a share of the Great California Land Company is going for as much as two dollars," Slocum said.

"I know. I'd buy it much cheaper, if I could, but Barclay refuses to sell to me."

That didn't ring true to Slocum. Barclay was selling to anyone who had even a worn hunk of bank scrip on him. Cuegant could have bought tons of the stock, for the right price, directly from the man issuing the certificates.

"You in the market for stock in the Great California Land Company then?" asked Slocum, an idea occurring to him. He watched Cuegant, but from the corner of his eye he saw Carrie stiffen. She wanted to protest, but Cuegant cut her off.

"Of course I am. We can swindle Emerson out of his land. He still doesn't understand the magnitude of the find. And if I tell him the few paltry diamonds found aren't worth the effort, he'll eventually sell. The Gold Trident is an albatross hanging around his neck."

"You'd lie to make a few dollars?" Slocum asked. "Or is it a lot of money?"

Cuegant smiled broadly. "You're a man of the world, I see, bloke. We can count on your support, can't we?"

"More than that," Slocum said. "I'm willing to sell you five thousand shares of stock in Barclay's land company. Since you balked at two dollars a share, I'll let it go for only one dollar a share."

Cuegant's reaction was everything he could have asked for. The DeBeers agent's face went white and his jaw dropped just enough to let Slocum know he had hit right on target.

"I don't have *that* kind of money."

"What would you have paid Barclay for shares? Five thousand?" Slocum prodded.

"Well, yes, that much." Cuegant squirmed now.

"What do I need to do to sign it over to you? Just put my John Hancock right here?" Slocum pulled out the five-thousand-share certificate Barclay had just given him for his "heroic" rescue.

"Gorblimey, you have the stock with you, I see."

"And you must have the money." Slocum reached over and patted Cuegant's pocket. A distinctively shaped lump betrayed the presence of a stack of greenbacks.

"I can give you diamonds in exchange," Cuegant said. "That's fair, since it is the source of our new wealth. You would come out ahead, of course."

"The jeweler, the one from San Francisco, might give a fair price for the stones, John," said Carrie. Her eyes shone like precious gems now. "You'd come out far ahead."

"Can't do that," Slocum said coldly. "Cheat you, I mean," he explained when Cuegant started to look relieved. "I'll let you pay me for the stock with the greenbacks. You can take your diamonds to the jeweler and get all the profit for yourself."

"John," Carrie Sinclair began.

"A moment," Slocum said. He faced down Ian Cuegant. And won. The man reluctantly peeled off five thousand dollars from the roll of greenbacks he carried. "Good. Let's go around the corner and find pen and ink and I'll sign over the stock to you." Slocum smiled wryly. "And remember, I'll be happy to sell you another ten thousand shares any time you want."

Ian Cuegant and Carrie Sinclair were strangely silent.

14

"For a man ready to get really rich, he sure does have a sour look," Slocum observed as Ian Cuegant walked away from the land office. They had officially recorded the exchange of the five thousand shares of stock Slocum held for a dollar a share. Seldom had he held so much money, and it made him feel cocky.

"John, you aren't looking at this right," Carrie Sinclair said earnestly. "You need to think of the future. You ought to consider how much longer you'll want to drift from town to town. Isn't settling down on your mind? Sometimes?" She looked up at him with her dazzling emerald eyes. A quick, nervous gesture moved a strand of coppery hair from her perfect oval face.

"I'm rich now," Slocum said. "Still have ten thousand shares Barclay gave me for services rendered in San Francisco."

"What were those services? That's a mighty handsome reward." She frowned. "For all that, five thousand shares for rescuing him was generous." Her tone spoke far more than the words. Carrie was not pleased that Barclay had been so overweeningly generous with shares in his company.

"He stands to make millions. What's a few dollars to a man like Astin Barclay?" Slocum asked, watching her carefully.

"You ought to use your money to buy even more shares in the Great California Land Company. Barclay is the only one left who can buy the mine from Emerson."

"You're giving up on your dream of getting what land Barclay doesn't own?"

She nodded solemnly. "I don't like it, but getting some of the pie is better than having none. He's a shrewd land speculator, that Mr. Barclay. He is the only one who can negotiate successfully with Mr. Emerson."

Slocum scratched his head as they stepped into the cool night-shrouded street. The ruckus down the street at the saloons had died down. Barclay had probably quit spending money for the night, leaving behind an army of drunk and dozing miners and locals. Lights winked off more and more, and even some of the hissing gas street lamps were being turned off as the marshal made his rounds.

That was about all he was good for, Slocum decided.

"Some things just don't measure up," Slocum said. "Can't make head nor tail of them."

"What might that be, John?" Carrie moved closer to him, her body warmth spreading along his left side as she hugged his arm close. He felt her firm breast under the crisply starched white blouse she wore. It distracted him a little.

He found the words. "Mrs. Rasmussen. She didn't really find a diamond in that turkey she butchered, but what was she doing in San Francisco? That's mighty far afield for her to travel."

"People from Oroville go into San Francisco periodically," she said. "Might be she has relatives there."

"Along the docks?" Slocum shrugged. "Might be."

"Come on. You're thinking too much," Carrie said.

"Afraid I'll strain myself?"

"Not that way," she said in a light voice. They walked, and Slocum found them heading for his hotel. That didn't bother him one little bit.

Upstairs in his room, Carrie closed the door and leaned back against it, her breasts rising and falling as her breathing increased. Slocum sat on the bed and watched her. She was a mighty handsome woman, one of the finest he had ever seen. He remembered what she had been hinting at while they were in the land office. A man couldn't float like a thistle on the wind forever. Even that thistle had to touch down and stick somewhere, sometime.

With the money he already had, it wouldn't be hard to buy a spread up north. Or maybe in East Texas. He'd always had a liking for the Piney Woods. It reminded him of Calhoun, Georgia, where he'd grown up.

"I want you, John," she said hotly. Her fingers worked frantically to unbutton her blouse. She tore off the useless garment and cast it aside as she dropped to the bed beside him.

He took her in his arms. She pressed hot and willing against him. Their lips met, a tentative touch, then a harder kiss backed with all the passion locked within both of them. Her tongue forced its way between his lips, then darted all around tormenting him.

She broke off the kiss to move back along the line of his jaw and nibble at his earlobe. As Carrie worked her magic on him, he worked to get out of his clothes. And then he found himself being helped. Her chest heaved under her frilly undergarment. Together they got it off to expose her luscious breasts to his lusting gaze.

He bent down and licked over both of the turgid nipples, tending to each in turn. She arched her back and thrust her chest forward, trying to force those succulent mounds into his mouth. He kept going the way he had started. A light nip here, a lick and kiss there.

"More, John, I want more. Give it all to me!" she moaned out as she lay back on the bed.

He reached over and unbuttoned her skirt. She lifted her hips from the bed so he could pull it free. Then he kissed her belly—and lower. She thrashed about as he nuzzled like a frisky horse in the tangled mat he found between her legs.

The pressures within his own body mounted and he could no longer restrain himself. He shoved back.

"No, don't!" she pleaded. "Let me." A naked Carrie Sinclair sat up on the bed and fumbled to get his jeans unbuttoned. He kicked free of his boots and pants, his manhood released from that cloth prison. He moaned when she took him in hand and began stroking. Then she lightly kissed just the tip of his shaft.

"Can't stand much more of that. Seeing you like this makes me want to—"

"Do it!" she cried. Carrie threw herself back on the bed and wantonly offered herself to him. He accepted the invitation. Dropping between her milky thighs, he moved forward. The tip of his manhood brushed across the coppery nest hiding her most intimate recesses. Then he sank deeply into her.

She arched her back and began rotating her hips in a wide circle, stirring him about within her tightness like a spoon in a mixing bowl. Together they moved, slowly at first, then with gathering speed and desire, until they were unable to hold back the dam burst of their mutual passions.

In a rush, Slocum was done. Carrie took a little longer. Afterward, they lay side by side, arms circling each other's sweaty body.

"I never thought I'd meet a man like you, John," Carrie said after a spell.

"A beautiful woman like you can have her pick of men."

The redhead snorted in disgust. "It never turns out that way, does it? You'd be surprised at the men who have disappointed me."

"That why you took up the crusade to stop the hydraulic mining?" he asked. "You thought a cause was better than a man?"

"Something like that, I suppose," she admitted. "But a cause is nowhere near as good as money. I'm coming to see that now." She rolled over and pressed her naked breasts into his chest so she could peer straight into his eyes. "Emerson will sell the mine. I know it. And Barclay is the one who can convince him."

"That worries me," Slocum said. "Emerson is a greedy man, from all accounts. He closed the Gold Trident as much because it was petering out as your protests. If he caught wind of another dime to be squeezed out of those rocks, he'd take it."

"He's heard all about the land rush, how Mr. Barclay's Great California Land Company is buying up the land. There's no way to prevent that. But he has an expert who might steer him in the wrong direction."

"Ian Cuegant?"

"Yes! Ian is an expert. He works for the largest diamond syndicate in the world. DeBeers controls eighty percent or more of all the precious stones mined. Emerson would never question Ian's opinion that there weren't any diamonds worth mining."

"But Emerson would still hold out for a huge amount, because Barclay is willing to pay it. Barclay's shown this already. He ought to have pretended to be disinterested, that he was doing Emerson a favor taking unproductive land off his hands for a song and a dance."

"Mr. Barclay's enthusiasm is not an easy thing to contain, but this is what makes him the only one able to get the land from Emerson.'' She stroked the hair on Slocum's chest with her fingertips. He felt tremors deep within his body at the teasing touch.

''So Cuegant will sell out his employer to make a fortune for himself?''

''I know you shouldn't trust anyone who is such an obvious double-crosser, John, but Ian doesn't really work for Emerson. He works for DeBeers and will simply get on a ship and head back to England. He's not crossing Emerson. He is only being loaned to Henry Emerson by DeBeers.''

''Wouldn't expect this DeBeers company to be happy with one of their own men lying to feather his own nest. Tarnishes their reputation a mite, wouldn't you say?''

''It'll work out. We'll all be rich. But Barclay needs the money to buy the mine from Emerson. Consider it an investment in your future. Buy more stock from Barclay.''

''I'm sitting on another ten thousand shares,'' Slocum said slowly, staring up into the darkness of the hotel room.

''Think how much you'd be worth if you owned twice that!''

''I'll think about it,'' Slocum said, rolling onto his side and pulling Carrie closer. ''Later.''

''There's Mrs. Rasmussen,'' Slocum said. ''Seems she and Barclay are having a confab.''

''He's buying her land. That's got to be it!'' Carrie Sinclair tugged at him, drawing him along the street like a dog on a leash. Slocum eyed the old woman and Barclay together and wondered what was actually going on. It didn't seem like a land deal as much as an argument. Barclay seemed to do a lot of that with a curious mix of people.

''Good morning, Mr. Barclay,'' Carrie said. ''We would like to speak to you about your land company.''

"I . . . I am involved in delicate negotiations at the moment with Mrs. Rasmussen."

"He won't pay me what my land's worth!" the woman shouted. "He knows what's on my property. It's all my dear departed Mr. Rasmussen left. He'd turn me out to starve, he would!"

Slocum heard a faint accent under the woman's ranting.

"My dear lady," Barclay said, "the diamond you found—the one you *thought* you found—turned out to be plain old rock. Worthless. We have no idea if there are *any* real diamonds on your land. I am speculating. I risk much."

"Sell him the mineral rights," Slocum said suddenly. "You get to stay on the land and do whatever you want. Raise vegetables, chickens, crops. But he gets to look for diamonds."

"That won't do, dearie," the old woman said in a broken voice. "I need to move on. Winters up here are too much for these tired, brittle bones. I want the money to move. But I won't give away my only legacy!"

"I'll buy your land, Mrs. Rasmussen," Carrie said loudly. "Whatever you ask, I'll give it to you!"

"Miss Sinclair, please," Barclay said. "This meddling is unprofessional. I protest!"

"Name your price," Carrie insisted to Mrs. Rasmussen. Slocum stepped away and watched the haggling go on. He drifted off and went across to the general store. He made his way through the piles of bolt fabrics and canned tomatoes until he found a small case with a half-dozen six-shooters displayed.

"What can I get for you?" asked the owner.

"Need slugs, gunpowder, wadding," Slocum said, drawing his Colt Navy and laying it on the counter. "About .31-caliber, unless firing it has worn the barrel a little bigger since last time I bought ammunition."

"I see," said the owner. He poked around and came up with what Slocum needed.

As Slocum paid, he asked the man, "See those folks across the street. You know 'em?"

"Who doesn't know Mr. Barclay. He's gonna make us all rich. The pretty lady with him is that hellion what closed down the mine. You want a box for all this?"

"All right," said Slocum. "What of the old woman? She's a relative of yours, isn't she?"

The man shrugged. "No kin of mine. Let her set up a table in here, but don't really know her. Been so many people flock to town, it's hard to keep track of all the new-comers. That's four dollars even. For another dollar I can throw in a can of gun oil."

Slocum turned down the offer of the oil, peeled off greenbacks from a roll in his shirt pocket, and pushed them across to the man.

"Thanks," Slocum said, going back across the street to where Carrie was finishing her deal with Mrs. Rasmussen.

"One thousand dollars it is, Mrs. Rasmussen."

Slocum saw the old woman tucking away a wad of scrip. She smiled broadly.

"Thank you, dearie. You're a good person." She glared at Barclay and Slocum and went off, humming "Sweet Betsy from Pike" to herself as she went.

"Now, Mr. Barclay, what do you say?" Carrie asked.

"You drive a ferocious bargain, Miss Sinclair. You re-alize shares of Great California Land Company are selling for five dollars each throughout Oroville now?"

"Very well," she said quickly. "I'll exchange the land I just purchased for two hundred fifty shares, so I can re-alize a profit of two hundred fifty dollars."

Slocum blinked. Five dollars a share? He held fifty thou-sand dollars worth of stock. Or ought he consider it to be even more? It made the paltry five thousand dollars he had weaseled out of Ian Cuegant seem insignificant.

"Yes, my dear, you are a ruthless one when it comes to bargaining. But I need that old woman's land. All that remains will be the purchase of the Gold Trident from Mr. Emerson." Barclay smiled, reached into his pocket, and pulled out a stock certificate. "Allow me to fill this out. Mr. Slocum can act as witness to the transaction."

"You might want to go to the land office," Slocum suggested. "The agent is a notary public."

"I am sure you will act fairly in this, John," said Carrie. "You would never want to see me swindled."

"Nor would you turn against me," Barclay said. "After all, Mr. Slocum, I have made you into a very wealthy man—with even more to come!" Barclay flourished his pen. For a moment, Slocum wondered where he would get the ink.

But Barclay had a small bottle stoppered in his coat pocket. He had been doing deals all morning long, and this was but one more. His pen scratched across the paper. He held it up to dry a moment in the sun, then handed it to Carrie Sinclair.

She took it as if he had handed her some religious relic.

"Thank you, Mr. Barclay." She took Slocum's arm and hurried off, a wide smile on her face. When they were out of earshot, she said to him, "John, this is wonderful! I made an instant profit!"

Before she could rattle on, she came to a halt. Blocking her path were four well-dressed men. Slocum recognized one as the town banker. The others had the look of San Francisco bankers about them.

"You!" said the Oroville banker. "You bought Mrs. Rasmussen's land! We had put in an offer for it!"

"Who are you talking about?" Slocum asked, moving forward a little so Carrie would be shielded. The men had the look of scorned lovers—or worse. Bankers who had been hornswoggled.

"The old woman went behind our backs. We—we are a consortium of bankers representing more than a quarter million dollars of assets. We wanted to buy, but the old woman sought another offer. That is unconscionable!"

"Illegal!" piped up another. "We are going to sue! We have lawyers who can force you to sell us the land!"

"Wait, wait," Carrie said, moving around Slocum. "I don't want any trouble. I hadn't realized Mrs. Rasmussen had been negotiating with you."

"Sell us the land!" demanded a third banker. "It'll be your head if you don't!"

"Don't threaten her," Slocum said in a cold voice. The banker moved back, disdain on his face mixed with just a tad of fear. Slocum was an intimidating figure, but greed drove the banker past fear of personal injury.

"We apologize if it sounded that way," the Oroville banker said. "But we will sue. We will tie up the deed for years if necessary."

"No, not that," Carrie said. Urgently she whispered to Slocum, "We need to get them on our side. Emerson would never settle if it looked as if Mr. Barclay could not finish a deal because of a lawsuit."

"What are you going to do?"

"Sirs," Carrie said, turning to them. "I traded the deed to Mr. Barclay for shares in the Great California Land Company. I will sell you the shares I just bought at a fair price."

"What's fair when speculators bid up the price minute by minute?" asked the whiskered banker who had remained silent to this point.

"Six dollars a share," she said. "For two hundred fifty shares." Seeing the bankers hesitant, Carrie rushed on. "It's what I received. I get nothing for my trouble."

"Buy the damned stock from her," said one San Francisco banker. "You know what we were offered earlier."

"Done," said the Oroville banker quickly, glaring at his partner. "My draft for fifteen hundred will be waiting for you at the bank. Bring the stock, and we will exchange it."

"When?" asked Carrie.

"Before noon."

"A deal," she said, thrusting out her hand. The banker hesitated, then took it and kissed the back. As if they were controlled by a single brain, the bankers stalked off, hunting more shares of Barclay's company.

"Won't be long before they own Barclay," Slocum opined.

"It might happen, but Mr. Barclay is a clever man," said Carrie. "But we need to talk, John. Those bankers weren't dangerous, but others might be. We need to be careful and watch our backs."

Slocum nodded. He pondered everything that had happened, the money changing hands, the ebb and flow of riches all around him.

"Go on back to your boardinghouse," he told her. "I'll be by in an hour or so to accompany you to the bank."

"Thank you, John. Thank you so much." She impetuously rose on tiptoe and kissed him on the cheek, then rushed off.

Slocum touched the spot Carrie had kissed, then remembered the night spent with her. He headed back to his hotel room. He had business of his own to conduct, and wanted it out of the way before they went to the bank.

15

"A Mason jar? Reckon I got one around somewhere. You fixin' to put up some vegetables?" joked the general store owner. He rummaged through a pile of boxes stacked precariously along one wall, found the right crate, and pulled out the glass jar. "You want a lid for it too?"

"Yes, thanks," said Slocum. He paid the dime for the jar and lid.

"Wait a minute," the man called as Slocum headed out the door. "You wantin' that for target practice? If you do, I got some old bottles out back you can have for nothing."

"This will do me just fine," Slocum said. He could see how the store owner had come to that conclusion after he'd bought ammunition for his Colt Navy earlier. Slocum looked around when it seemed as if he had stepped into a furnace. The late afternoon heat wore down the people in Oroville, keeping them inside as much as possible. A few horses tethered outside saloons wobbled, suffering in the heat. He saw how few of the water troughs along the main street had been filled. The land rush had taken everyone's attention away from simple chores, focusing the people on getting rich owning land with diamonds hidden under the dirt.

He walked slowly down the street, returning to his hotel room. He fumbled in his pocket, pulled out a small, lumpy cornmeal bag, and shoved it into his jar once the door clicked shut behind him. A few quick turns sealed the lid down tight. Jar under his arm, Slocum slipped out the window of his second-story room, dropped to the ground, and headed for the livery stable.

The owner snored loudly in the tack room, the rattling echoes loud enough to wake the dead. His young helper, probably his son from the resemblance, should have been working. He had crawled into the hayloft for an afternoon siesta too. Slocum borrowed a shovel used for mucking and went to the corner of the stall, where his horse nuzzled him, hoping for a carrot or lump of sugar.

"Sugar I've got, but nothing more. Sorry, fella," Slocum said. As the horse ruminated on the few lumps of sugar given him, Slocum dug a hole in the hard-packed dirt at the rear of the stall. When he had a hole a foot deep, he dropped in the jar and its contents. A few quick shovel loads of dirt refilled the hole. Straw covered all evidence that he had hidden anything at all.

"Feel better about this. You stand guard, and I'll see you get a box of sugar cubes," he promised the horse. Slocum ducked back out the rear of the stable, looking around. He had felt eyes watching him wherever he went for the past few hours. Playing it safe seemed prudent. He made his way back to the rear of the hotel, crawled up on a water barrel, then jumped to catch at the second-story windowsill. He pulled himself up and over the ledge, tumbling into his room.

Heaving a sigh, Slocum stretched out on the bed. The seething heat wore him down like he was a piece of soft iron under a determined rasp file. He drifted off to a troubled sleep filled with gunmen shooting at him, huge pits opening under his feet, and a curious sense of abandonment he hadn't felt since he'd learned his brother Robert had been killed at Little Roundtop.

He rolled over and clutched at the thin feather pillow. In his half sleep he imagined the pillow turned into Carrie Sinclair, then into a snake, slithering away. Slocum came awake with a start, sweat drenching him.

His hand went for the Colt on the bedside table. A rifle butt crashed down on his wrist, knocking his hand away painfully.

Slocum wasted no time trying to figure out if this was still part of his nightmare. The pain was real enough to send him rolling in the opposite direction. The sudden shift in direction sent him crashing into another man's legs, bowling him over. Slocum swung a fist and landed it clumsily on the downed man's head. Cursing the numbness in his hand from the rifle butt, Slocum rolled over and used his elbow on the man's face. Blood spurted all over Slocum's sleeve, the man's broken nose spewing like a fountain.

"Damn him! He busted my nose!" cried the man on the floor.

As the man reached for his injured nose, Slocum grabbed for the man's fallen six-gun. Hand still not fully functioning, Slocum fumbled but still got the six-shooter lifted. He fired point-blank into the second man's chest as he came around.

The man wore a bandanna as a mask, but his eyes went wide. Then it was Slocum's turn to let shock and surprise wash over him. He had fired but nothing had happened. His shot ought to have taken the man's life. Instead, a tiny patch directly over the heart burned from partially ignited gunpowder and wadding.

Slocum slugged the man with the broken nose, levered himself to his feet, and stumbled from the room, leaving behind both would-be killers—or were they kidnappers?

Slocum was still groggy from sleep, though his head cleared rapidly as he took the stairs down to the lobby two at a time. The clerk looked up, startled at the sight of a man without boots but holding a six-gun.

"Something wrong, Mr. Slocum?"

Slocum considered asking the clerk to fetch the marshal, then decided against it. The law man would have to form a committee to study the problem, then poll the citizens of Oroville to see if it merited his attention. By the time he got around to doing anything, an entire company of road agents could have passed through town.

"Nothing. Just had a nightmare."

"It's the heat. You might go over to the Oriental Saloon. Heard tell they got some ice. A cold beer is the thing to fix you up."

"I'll think on it," Slocum said. He checked the six-shooter and found the bullet had partially fired, jamming the barrel. If he had tried to fire it a second time, it might have blown his hand off. Rather than try to clean it and bore out the lead plug in the barrel, Slocum hefted it as a club and went back upstairs.

He hesitated at the door to his room, then spun inside ready for a fight. He found a puddle of drying blood and nothing more to show he had run off his unwanted visitors. Tossing the worthless six-gun onto the bed, Slocum strapped on his own trusty Colt Navy, then pulled on his boots.

A cold beer seemed like a mighty fine idea about now.

Rather than going out through the lobby, Slocum chose the back stairs. He sorted out the flashing impressions of the two men in his room. Both were familiar, but the only one he could positively identify was the one whose nose he had broken.

He was the second of the inept pair that had tried to waylay Astin Barclay on the road to San Francisco—and the surviving member after they had kidnapped Barclay.

"Should have finished him off too," Slocum decided as he stepped off the rear stairs and into the dusty alley behind the hotel. He never felt the rifle butt that crashed into the back of his head, knocking him facedown into the dust.

Slocum tried to guess how long he had been unconscious. From the pain in his head, he thought it might have been a considerable time. There was no way under the sun he could have built up so much pain in just a few seconds. Sorting through the sources of torment convinced him he was being knocked about in the rear of a wagon, his hands tied behind his back and his feet securely tied.

Curling his knees up stopped some of the side-to-side motion that battered him constantly. He forced his back against the side of the wagon and sat up enough to see two men in the wagon seat. Both wore bandannas as masks, but he immediately recognized them. He would have had to be blind to miss the driver's blood-soaked bandanna. His busted nose still leaked blood.

Slocum took scant pleasure in that. His hands had gone numb, and he doubted he could kick off his boots to free his feet. A bump sent him rolling to the other side of the wagon. He tried to get a better look at the second man, the one with a seared vest where the gunpowder had burned but no bullet had ripped out his heart. The man looked familiar, but Slocum couldn't positively identify him bouncing around the way he did.

"There's the mine," said the driver. "What we do with him now?"

The second man—the one Slocum couldn't identify—said nothing, but simply pointed down toward the gorge.

"Aw, no, that's too damn cruel."

The man reached over and tweaked the driver's broken

nose. The yelp of pain and the string of curses turned the air blue.

"I can do it. He deserves it, but I still say it's danged cruel."

Slocum kicked hard, got his shoulders over the top of the wagon sides, and tried to roll out. A strong hand reached back and grabbed him.

"None of that now," came the muffled order as the second kidnapper shoved Slocum down.

Rather than struggle futilely, Slocum subsided and tried to work on the ropes around his wrists. He found a nail poking up through the wagon bed, and began picking at the hemp binding him. A strand or two would part, then nothing. Another strand, a bit more hope he might break the ropes from sheer strength, then hope fled.

The wagon ground to a halt and the men jumped out. They came around, grabbed Slocum, and carried him between them like a sack of potatoes.

"What are you going to do?" Slocum asked. If they had wanted to kill him, they could have done it outright back in his hotel room.

"You got paid a hell of a lot of money," said the one with the broken nose. He rubbed his bloody bandanna and tried to stop a new flood. "We want it. Where'd you put it?"

"How do you know?" asked Slocum. He dismissed the one he had repeatedly beaten up and fixed his eyes on the other man. He was familiar. Too familiar. The man's eyes mirrored Slocum's realization of whom he faced.

Ian Cuegant ripped off his mask and sneered. "You have five thousand of my money, you do, mate. I want it back."

"What's wrong? Couldn't sell the stock I sold you?"

"Price was too high. If it hadn't been for *her*, I'd never have bought it from you."

"But you can get rich," Slocum taunted. He got a hard

fist driven into his belly. Doubled over, he coughed and tried to get his breath back.

"The money. It wasn't on you. We looked. You didn't hide it in your room."

"If you'd found it, would you have left me alone?" Slocum asked.

"No. I want to make sure you don't meddle anymore where you don't belong."

Slocum was dragged along between the two men. He twitched and jerked, trying to worry another few strands of rope free. The nail in the wagon had started it, but he needed time—time he wasn't likely to be given. When they reached the edge of the steep gorge gnawed out by the hydraulic mining, they dropped him.

He kicked and tried to work his feet free. No slack. He rolled onto his side and looked up at Cuegant.

"You make this sound personal. I'll tell you where your money is."

"Good, where is it?" said the broken-nosed man.

Slocum saw the look on Cuegant's face. He had seen it before on men whipping themselves up into a killing mood. No amount of money would sate this man's hunger to see John Slocum die.

"You missed it because I put it in my bedroll. It's with my tack over at the livery stable."

"Want me to go look, Mr. Cuegant?"

"Yeah, go on, but I think he's lying."

"I don't want to waste my time goin' back to town," the man whined. "Not if it's a fool's errand."

"For you, any errand would be thus," said Cuegant. "If we want to save you the bloody ride, we ought to be certain he's not fibbing to us, now shouldn't we?" Cuegant caught up Slocum and whirled him around so his back crashed smack into the muzzle of the water cannon. The monitor felt cold, and Slocum stared out into space, down into the gorge.

"Fasten him in place," Cuegant ordered.

"What you fixin' to do?"

"Get to the truth." Cuegant stood back, arms crossed on his chest, and sneered at Slocum as his henchman tied Slocum into place in front of the monitor.

"The money's where I said," Slocum declared coldly. He wasn't going to show any of the fear chewing at his guts. He wouldn't give Cuegant the pleasure. The cold bore of the monitor promised watery death if Cuegant turned it on. Slocum had seen the way the water cannon ripped away solid rock a hundred yards away on the far side of the gorge. A human body stuck in that stream would be turned into a bloody spray.

"Is it, now?"

"If I'm lying and you kill me, you'll never find the money," said Slocum.

"But the pleasure of watching you squirm might compensate," Cuegant said.

"Wait, Mr. Cuegant. *I* want my cut of the money!"

"Shut up, you worm. Get up the hill and start the engines. I want just a little water pressure at first. Then build it to full."

"But he'll . . ." The man's voice trailed off when he realized Cuegant's plan. He touched the busted nose Slocum had given him; then his demeanor hardened. "He done kilt a good friend," he said. "You're right, Mr. Cuegant. He don't deserve to live, money or no."

"Go!"

"What's in this for you, Cuegant?" asked Slocum. "There's plenty of money to go around, even for a greedy bastard like you."

Cuegant laughed harshly. "There's never enough for

me," he said. "I have other—how do you Americans say it?—fish to fry."

Slocum winced as the first stream of water crashed into his back. It bent him away from the monitor nozzle, causing his spine to arch painfully.

"Capital. The pumps are going. It won't be long now," Cuegant said.

"The money's not in my bedroll."

"I know. I looked there already," Cuegant said. "Revenge would be much sweeter if I had found the money, but it is not necessary for me to enjoy your death fully." Cuegant stepped back and shouted, "Full pressure!"

"Revenge? What've I ever done to you?" Slocum gasped as the water pressure increased until he was sure it would break his back. Then the flow dropped to a trickle, allowing him to relax.

"What's going on? Turn it on full-stream!" bellowed Cuegant.

"Mr. Cuegant, there's somethin' powerful wrong here. I don't know what it is."

"Fix it!"

"I don't know how to run this danged hunk of machinery. There's dials and steam comin' out. I think the boiler's busted."

"The boiler is perfectly operational. I saw it earlier," Cuegant said.

Slocum sagged against the ropes holding him on the monitor. He let his head fall forward, but he was not stunned. He frantically worked on the rope, using his fingernails to tear one tough strand of rope after another where the nail had begun the work.

He jerked when a *pop!* of water belched from the monitor, then sagged again when the water flow reduced to a trickle.

"You fool," grumbled Cuegant. "Start the monitor!"

"Cain't," came the plaintive answer. "This is beyond me."

Cuegant saw how Slocum slumped. He kicked Slocum hard, then struggled up the steep hill toward the engine and pump where his henchman worked so ineffectively. The instant the Britisher vanished from sight, Slocum began sawing the rope back and forth on the edge of the monitor. Its slick steel barrel afforded little in way of cutting surface, but it was tougher than his fingernails.

Scraping harder and harder, Slocum felt blood begin to trickle down over his hands as the rope abraded his flesh. Uphill he heard Cuegant cursing volubly as he worked to get the pump working that would send the high-pressure column of water through Slocum's body like a liquid cannonball.

He hopped, trying to swing to one side of the nozzle or the other. They had bound him too well for that. He kicked and tried to get his feet up to roll backward, hoping to evade the water this way. He couldn't. Slocum fell back into place, staring into the twilight beginning to hide the distant bank like a death shroud.

The monitor began to quiver as water pressure mounted. He heard the chuff-chuff of the engine powering the hydraulic cannon, and Cuegant's triumphant cry.

Slocum sawed harder, feeling friction mount between rope and metal barrel. The monitor shook and a stream of water poked at him. Then came the ear-splitting rush of full-force water capable of tearing away tons of solid rock in a few seconds.

16

Slocum felt the skin on his wrists yield—along with the rope. He was lifted and thrown forward as the water surged from the monitor. Slocum slammed facedown in mud below the monitor, starting to slide toward the gorge. He tried to get his feet under him, but they were still tied. He slued around, grabbing for any purchase.

Above his head the monitor roared out its deep-throated song of death. Cuegant had not set the screws on it; the water cannon began bucking and sending its deadly torrent in all directions. Struggle as he might, Slocum couldn't get any grip. He slid faster and faster down the slope toward the hundred-foot drop into the gorge.

Just as he was sure he was a goner, a sharp yank on his arm halted his descent. He wiped mud from his eyes and saw the severed end of the rope around his left wrist snagged on a rock. Precarious though it was, Slocum managed to grab with his right hand and pull himself a few inches up the muddy slope. A hand on the rock snagging the rope gave a bit more security. Then he got his feet up where he could work on the ropes. It took several minutes before he freed himself.

Then he found a new danger—or was it only an old one?

"He got free, I tell you," growled Ian Cuegant.

"How could he, Mr. Cuegant? It looks like the force of the water blowed him smack out into the gorge."

"Fool. Hunt for him. Show me his bloody corpse!"

Slocum wiped more mud and water from his face. He was ten yards below them. It wouldn't take Cuegant but a few seconds to come this way. There wasn't anything Slocum could do to stop him if the man got him in his sights.

Like putting his toes into a stirrup, he kicked hard and formed footholds for his boots. Slocum made his way up the slope until he found a part that had somehow been spared the full force of water running downhill. He made better time, coming up even with the monitor almost ten yards away.

Of Cuegant he saw no trace. The other kidnapper ineffectually poked around, trying to see anything in the gathering twilight. Slocum used the darkness and the roar of the monitor to hide his approach.

He tapped the man on the shoulder.

As the outlaw turned, Slocum slugged him. He felt more cartilage yield under his fist. The kidnapper struggled, fell back, and lost his footing in the mud. Slocum tried to follow him, only to slip himself. He fell, got back to his feet, and found himself facing death again.

"Don't go messin' with me," the outlaw said, his voice shrill. Blood ran down his lip. He spat and swiped at the new injury. But his other hand held the wood handle on the monitor, ready to swing it around and blast Slocum off his muddy perch on the side of the hill.

"Cuegant is getting you in a heap of trouble," Slocum said, edging around. The monitor had to have some limit to how far it would swing. The man jerked on the water cannon and caused it to follow. Its stream was still between Slocum and the gorge, but getting closer. A touch of even one side of the torrents of water roaring from the monitor would be his end.

Slocum had always thought he would die with a bullet in his gut—or in his back. Never had he considered a cannonade from a hydraulic mining monitor.

"He's a smart man," the outlaw said.

"Smart?" Slocum laughed harshly. "Your partner's dead. You're all banged up. The only way Cuegant is smart is that he lets others take his licks for him. Hope you're getting paid well for it."

"I am," the man said. His tiny brain fastened on the one thing he understood. "Where'd you really hide that money Mr. Cuegant gave you?"

"He's rich. Why's he worry about a few thousand dollars?"

"That's a powerful lot of money," the man said. Slocum saw the other man's attention shift to spending so much money. He dug in his toes and launched himself. Crashing into the barrel of the monitor was almost as big a shock as getting shot. The powerful stream caused the monitor to jerk around when Slocum knocked it free of the outlaw's grip. For a moment, Slocum hung on, then let the whipping water cannon toss him in the direction he wanted.

He crashed hard into the man, pinning him to the muddy ground.

Slocum cocked his fist back, ready to punch again. He held back when he saw the crazy angle of the man's head. Slocum had been swung around by the monitor. The lash had also caught the kidnapper in the side of the head, breaking his neck like a chicken bone.

Throwing himself to one side to sit on the ground, Slocum panted harshly. The danger had passed. Better, he saw the ebony butt of his own Colt Navy thrust into the man's holster. Slocum grabbed the six-shooter and felt better for its familiar bulk in his hand.

Before hunting Cuegant, Slocum searched the dead man for some clue as to what was going on. He found a pair of greenbacks in a shirt pocket and nothing more. Slocum tucked them back in. It wouldn't be enough for a headstone, but it might convince the Oroville undertaker to give something more formal than the potter's field.

Wiping water from his face, Slocum started upslope in the direction of the pumps and steam engine powering the monitor. The equipment towered over him, forming a maze he searched with increasing caution. He saw nothing of Ian Cuegant. The man had been with his dead partner down at the water cannon, but had left. Where'd he go?

On impulse, Slocum reached up and pulled a lever that cut off the pump feeding the monitor. Then he turned off the steam engine. It wound down with a loud hiss and whine. The sudden silence, along with the gathering twilight gray, hit Slocum like a hammer blow. He had not realized how loud the roar of the water cannon was until it stopped.

Walking around the huge pump and its rocker arm, he hunted for any trace of Cuegant. He saw nothing. The wagon with its two horses that had brought them to the hydraulic mine stood abandoned a few yards away. Slocum went to the scene of the last shootout, searching the foreman's cabin—or what little was left of it—and the stable.

He considered calling out a challenge. Whatever Cuegant had against him surpassed merely doing him out of the five thousand dollars. Too much of what went on in Oroville needed answering. Slocum smiled wryly when he realized some answers were being provided. Both men who had tried to waylay Astin Barclay on the road to San Francisco were dead.

"They also gave Carrie the diamonds she took to San Francisco," he said, growling. That didn't fit well. If men like those had diamonds, why pass them along to Carrie

Sinclair? They were greedy and not too bright. It didn't take more than a tot of good sense to know they could have sold the diamonds themselves, even if they had stolen them.

But where would they have stolen them? Slocum didn't know. Barclay had diamonds that sparked jewelers' interest—like the jeweler who had suddenly relocated from San Francisco to set up shop in Oroville, who had whipped up interest in hunting for more. But even old Mrs. Rasmussen hadn't found a diamond, in spite of her loud declarations she had.

"Where are you, Cuegant? You can answer a powerful lot of questions for me." Six-gun in a steady hand, Slocum went prowling. It took almost a half hour before he heard noise in the woods to the east of the mining camp. Another five minutes passed before Slocum admitted the sound came from a human rather than some critter out hunting for an easy evening meal.

Scaling a pine tree, Slocum crawled out on a high limb and lay flat on it, arms and legs dangling down. He pushed up slightly when he saw a dark shape moving along the path beneath the tree. Slocum had learned patience during the war. As a sniper, he'd often waited for hours before taking a single shot that might determine the outcome of a battle. That persistence aided him now.

The man came along the trail, hesitated, looked around. A faint ray of moonlight from the quarter moon slanted through the canopy of trees and illuminated Cuegant's face. The man seemed perplexed. He twisted around in a full circle, his pistol shining brightly. As before, he carried a derringer.

After another few seconds of standing stock-still, Cuegant walked directly under Slocum's perch. Like a springing puma, Slocum dove down and crashed into Cuegant. He knocked the man to the ground. Seeing Cuegant still clinging to the derringer, Slocum grabbed for it to wrest it from his grip.

"You!" Cuegant grated out in surprise. He swung his left hand like a meaty club. The blow knocked Slocum to the side of the path, giving Cuegant time enough to scuttle away like a crab. He lifted his derringer and fired, but Slocum attacked again, coming in below the man's arm.

Slocum's shoulder knocked Cuegant to the ground. This time Slocum measured his attack and sent a fist into the Britisher's gut. It was surprisingly hard and Cuegant didn't stay down. He kicked and tangled Slocum's feet, giving him time to regain both balance and wind.

"You just won't die, will you?" Cuegant panted, aiming the derringer at Slocum. "This will be the last time you—"

Slocum threw a handful of pine needles and dirt into the air. He missed Cuegant's face, but obscured the man's aim enough to avoid the heavy slug that ripped through the night. Slocum considered using his own six-shooter, and then knew if he did he might kill Cuegant. He wanted answers to a passel of hard questions only the DeBeers agent could provide.

Derringer empty, Cuegant turned and fled in the direction of the hydraulic mine. Slocum wasn't as fast a sprinter as Cuegant, but he had more stamina. He overtook him near the now-silent steam engine and water pump. Reaching out, Slocum shoved hard and sent Cuegant crashing to the ground. Slocum overran him, skidded to a halt, and wheeled around.

Cuegant got to his feet, hands balled into fists. "Marquis of Queensberry rules are out of the question, aren't they? Bare knuckles it will be."

Slocum still had the option of using his Colt. He smiled crookedly. This was going to be a pleasure. He stepped up, ready for the fight. Cuegant's fist sailed past his ear. Slocum drove a quick left and right into the man's midsection. Before, that belly had been tight. This time, Slocum felt the muscles give under the one-two onslaught.

He stepped back and caught a light blow on the side of his head. It staggered but did not stun him.

"I can give as well as I receive, old man," said Cuegant, moving in because he thought he had Slocum. He quickly found out Slocum still packed quite a wallop. Two more blows to the belly caused Cuegant to wheeze and step away to gather his senses. Slocum didn't permit him time to recover.

A flurry of blows, none too hard but all landing, brought Cuegant to his knees. Slocum stepped away. The rules of boxing required a ten-second count. Slocum judged his distance, then launched a kick that ended in the middle of Cuegant's chest. The man let out a shriek of unadulterated pain and fell to the ground, clutching himself and making mewling noises as he tried to get wind back into his tortured lungs.

"No more bullshit, Cuegant," Slocum said. He grabbed the man by the hair and dragged him to a sitting position. "I've got questions, and you've got answers. We can trade them."

"No, won't say anything," Cuegant said. Slocum hit him on the side of the jaw, knocking his head around.

"I don't want to mess up your good looks, but I'm willing to turn your face to horse meat unless you tell me what I want."

"What?" the man gasped out. "What do you want to know?"

"Why'd DeBeers send you halfway around the world? It doesn't make sense. Even a telegram to Europe wouldn't have brought you this fast."

"Was in Mexico," Cuegant rasped out. He smiled around the blood oozing from his cut mouth. "But you have it all wrong, bucko."

"What's that?"

"I don't work for DeBeers."

"You mean you work for Emerson?"

"He hired me," came the evasive answer. Slocum heard more mystery than truth in Cuegant's words. He hit him again.

"All right, all right. I'll tell you. I work for Emerson. He hired me because he thinks I'm a DeBeers bloke. It's all a scam, a fraud, though. I tell him what we want him to think, not the truth. Never that." Cuegant laughed, then coughed up blood. He spat. "You broke something inside me, you did, Slocum."

"I'll break a lot more. Keep talking. You're in cahoots with Barclay, aren't you? You're supposed to lie to Emerson and tell him there aren't any diamonds in the petered-out gold mine?"

"An interesting take on it," Cuegant said. "You really don't have the ghost of an idea what this is about, do you, old man?"

"Tell me. Now."

"It's all so simple. You see—" Cuegant stiffened and then keeled over when the bullet caught him in the side of the head. One temple had a tiny hole. The other showed an exit hole the size of a silver dollar.

Slocum went into a crouch, drew, and had his Colt Navy aimed in the direction of the shot before he even realized Ian Cuegant was not going to answer any more questions.

From the sound of the gunshot, Slocum reckoned he faced a man with a rifle. And a damned good shot too to kill Cuegant so cleanly. But where was the hidden sniper? Darkness clutched all the buildings, and Slocum had not seen the orange tongue from the rifle muzzle, even from the corner of his eye.

Backing off, he worked his way around the steam engine and toward the foreman's cabin. Lou Morgan had left it in good shape. Now only one wall still stood, but this gave Slocum a little shelter from new rifle fire. Or so he thought. A bullet ripped away a piece of the wall not six inches from his nose. Slocum dropped to his belly, twisted, and fired twice in the direction of the stables. This time he had seen the foot-long tongue of fire from the sniper's rifle.

"That you, Barclay?" called Slocum. "You tying up the loose ends by killing your partners?"

Slocum got no answer. He hadn't expected any. He slithered like a snake and got to the bunkhouse door. Using the half-buried bunkhouse for shelter, he judged distances. It didn't look good for him to make a frontal assault. The gunman was a good shot—better than Slocum would have thought under these conditions.

He had misjudged Barclay—it had to be Astin Barclay. Who else stood to gain from bilking Emerson out of the mine? The Great California Land Company owned all the surrounding land, and would soon own even the hydraulic mine. The diamonds would be his for the taking.

Slocum climbed to the top of the hill where the bunkhouse had been partially buried. Getting ready, he made a quick run through the night, found the crate he remembered at the corner of the stables, then launched himself. He fell heavily onto the roof of the stable.

He immediately regretted his impetuosity. Holes appeared all around him as Barclay shot through the roof. Slocum reduced the area where Barclay might wing him by standing up. As he did, he felt the flimsy roof under him yield. He tried to move, only to find himself falling into the stable amid a clutter of wood and thatching used for makeshift shingles.

He hit, the impact jarring him so hard he lost his balance. Slocum rolled and brought his six-shooter up, ready for action, only to find the stables empty. Again Barclay had shown more presence of mind than Slocum would have thought possible.

After firing through the roof, Barclay had hightailed it.

Slocum took a few seconds to check the stalls to be sure he wasn't going to get backshot, then slipped out the door. Muddy tracks showed the course taken by the escaping man. Dropping to his knee, Slocum saw the imprint of a left boot with a peculiar crescent cut in the middle of the heel. Then he found a right boot imprint with the same.

"Boot heels are custom-made," he decided.

Slocum made his way along the trail, going into the woods. The sound of a horse caused him to rush forward— almost to his death.

Three quick rounds buzzed past his head. Barclay had spooked his own horse to draw Slocum out. And it had worked. Slocum felt like a complete greenhorn underestimating Astin Barclay in this fashion.

He returned fire, shooting for the thicket where the rifle shots had almost claimed his life. Nothing. No sound, no movement, nothing. Slocum circled, keeping to shadows and trying to avoid stepping into the wan silver light cast by the rising moon.

"I'll be damned," Slocum said. He had been outfoxed again. Barclay had shot at him, then cleared out fast. Back in the direction of the mine, Slocum heard the clatter of wagon wheels and the whinnying protest of the two horses as they were whipped into motion.

Barclay had chased off his own horse as a decoy, then doubled back and claimed the wagon Cuegant and his henchman had used to bring Slocum to the mine.

On foot, angry at his own carelessness and stupidity, Slocum headed back for Oroville. It was a long walk and he had serious business with Astin Barclay.

17

Slocum was footsore and angrier than a wet hen by the time he reached Oroville. He stomped along the dusty main street as dawn pinked the eastern sky. A cool breeze kept the sweat from his face, but the rest of his body protested every movement. His legs hurt from the long hike, and worse than the blisters and aches, he was furious at himself for somehow getting lost twice on the way back when he had tried to take shortcuts and left the deeply rutted road.

A single saloon halfway down the street still roared with boisterous business. Slocum headed for it, thinking to get a drink or two under his belt before he found Barclay and wrung his neck. As he entered, he saw the target of his ire sitting at a table in the back of the saloon. A half-dozen men surrounded him, all dickering over sales of stock in Barclay's company.

"What'll it be? You look to have a powerful thirst," the barkeep said. He dropped a polishing rag and felt under the bar for a dirty glass and a bottle half-filled with a murky substance that had never been within five hundred miles of Kentucky, no matter what the faded label proclaimed.

"Whiskey," Slocum said, eyeing the concoction with some disdain. Right now, he wasn't feeling too fussy about the kind of alcohol he put into his belly. He knocked back the shot of trade whiskey, made a face at the heavy gunpowder taste, then indicated he wanted another. The bartender silently poured it.

"How long's he been here?" Slocum asked, pointing in Barclay's direction.

"Mr. Barclay's been here for a couple hours, maybe longer. He surely does bring the crowd with him. I got a hundred shares of the Great California Land Company myself," the barkeep said proudly. "How many shares do you own?"

"I need to have words with him," Slocum said, finishing the second drink. He stomped over to Barclay's table and stared down at the portly man. Barclay was flushed and his pockets bulged from the greenbacks he had stuffed there. A half-dozen pens and a couple of empty ink bottles sat on the table, mute testimony to how much stock he had recently sold in his company.

"Mr. Slocum, good morning! Might I offer you a drink, although it is just an hour before breakfast?"

"You backshooter," Slocum snarled. The din around Barclay's table died, and the men who had so eagerly crowded close now backed off. They heard death in Slocum's accusation.

"What are you saying, my good man?" Barclay's face showed a tinge of fear, and his hands shook like he had some strange ague. He had to force them flat on the table to keep from openly quaking.

"You killed Cuegant and tried to kill me." Slocum's anger built. He had to keep his own hand from shaking, but it was more like a racehorse ready to run than from any fear. He wanted to kill something. All it would take was a single swift move to his cross-draw holster and the Colt Navy would come out, cock, and fire in one single action.

"Whatever are you saying? When was this? Where?

What happened?'' Barclay looked around in desperation, as if he thought someone in the crowd would come to his aid.

''Out at the Gold Trident, hours back. You stranded me there.''

''The mine?'' Barclay blinked, and his mouth opened and closed twice without any more words coming out.

Slocum's resolve began to fade. How a man who got this flustered could have cold-bloodedly fired through Cuegant's head bothered him. Still, it might have been a lucky shot, although the rest of the pursuit had shown cunning surpassing anything Barclay might be capable of.

''Where have you been?'' Slocum demanded.

''Why, here, in Oroville. All night. I started yesterday afternoon raising money to buy Mr. Emerson's mine, and have been hard at work ever since. All night!''

''You haven't left Oroville?''

''No!''

Slocum almost believed him.

''That's right, Mr. Slocum,'' said one of the men at the edge of the silent crowd of onlookers. ''I been followin' him round all night long. He's been buyin' me and everyone else drinks. A real generous gent, Mr. Barclay.''

Slocum saw others nodding in agreement. There was no way they would have spoken up to save Barclay's bacon if it hadn't been true.

''You weren't out at the mine?'' Slocum asked Barclay.

''Not recently. Not for several days, actually.''

Barclay yelped as Slocum knelt, grabbed him around the ankles, and yanked. The portly man's boot heels were smooth except where one showed a nail worn through the leather. The curious imprint Slocum had noted on both of the bushwhacker's boots were missing. Slocum dropped Barclay's feet to the floor, thinking hard.

''What is this all about, Mr. Slocum? What's this about Cuegant being killed?'' Panic tinged Barclay's voice now, more than before when he thought Slocum was ready to kill him.

"Cuegant and one of the men who grabbed you knocked me out and took me out to the hydraulic mine to kill me," Slocum said. Barclay went pale under the sheen of sweat on his round face. "I killed one, then someone shot Cuegant before I could find out who he really worked for."

"H-he worked for DeBeers," stammered Barclay.

"No, he didn't," Slocum said. "He came up the coast on the ship from Mexico, not from England as he led everyone to believe, though I think he *was* British." Slocum pinned Barclay to the chair with his cold green gaze. "He worked for you, didn't he? Ian Cuegant?"

"Please, sir, this is no place to discuss such sensitive matters. I don't know what's going on!"

Slocum believed Barclay this time. His mind raced, trying to put all the pieces together. Barclay and Cuegant worked together to fleece Emerson. But there was another player in the game. Slocum ran his fingers over the gold pin he had found when Barclay had been kidnapped.

He swung around and stalked out. A collective gasp passed through the crowd as he stepped into the street, now dim with dawn light. Slocum headed for the jeweler's shop next to the land office. He wasn't too surprised to find the man hard at work, already appraising stones brought to him. The old man looked up, for a moment not seeming to recognize Slocum.

"You'll have to wait your turn," he said carefully. "All these people are ahead of—"

"This your work?" Slocum dropped the gold pin onto the counter in front of the jeweler. Slocum read the answer, although the man lied and denied it. "Who'd you sell it to?"

"I just told you, I've never seen it before."

"The man who bought it killed Ian Cuegant tonight. I'm sure of it."

"What!" The jeweler jumped back as if he had been burned. "No, you're wrong. He can't be dead! Ian?"

"He is. Shot through the head. By the man who dropped this." Slocum took a stab in the dark at Cuegant's true killer. It made sense that the same man who had ordered Barclay's kidnapping must have killed Cuegant.

"I know nothing about this," the jeweler said. The old man ran his gnarled hands through his thinning gray hair, then made frantic shooing motions. "Get out. All of you, please leave. Now! I am doing no more appraisals today. Go!"

Slocum went along with the half-dozen men who had gathered to have their rocks examined. He stopped one who had been crowded into the jeweler's shop with a bag of worthless rocks and asked, "What's a share in the Great California Land Company selling for now?"

"I paid ten dollars a share last night, but this morning I heard tell it's going for up to twelve," the man boasted. "I made twenty percent profit in just one day!"

Slocum said no more. He saw the jeweler hurrying down the alley beside his shop, intent on hightailing it. Slocum followed carefully, not wanting the man to see him. The jeweler was obviously worried that Slocum—or someone—would follow. He tried doubling back and several other tactics that did nothing to throw Slocum off the trail. Interested in where his quarry sought refuge, Slocum was in no hurry to close in on the man.

Where the jeweler led him took Slocum by surprise.

Slocum stood and stared as the old man rapped insistently on the window in the boardinghouse. Carrie Sinclair came to the window. The jeweler moved closer and spoke with great animation to the lovely redhead for a few minutes. Carrie chewed her lower lip, then burst into tears.

Whatever Slocum had been expecting, it wasn't this. He considered walking over and finding out exactly what was going on from both the old jeweler and Carrie. Then he decided Astin Barclay was a better source.

He spun and returned to the saloon where Barclay had been holding court. The room was empty except for the sleepy barkeep dozing on the bar. He shook himself awake when he heard the clicking of Slocum's boots on the wood floor.

"Back for another round?" the bartender asked, rubbing sleep from his eyes.

"Barclay. Where'd he go?"

The barkeep scratched his head, then shrugged. Slocum hurried from the saloon, intent on finding Barclay. But everywhere he looked, he just missed the man. As Barclay rushed through Oroville, he sold stock in the Great California Land Company. It was as if he was making one last great big effort to fleece everyone before heading for the high country.

"You see Astin Barclay today?" he called to the owner of the livery stable. Slocum couldn't tell if any horses were gone from the stalls. He checked his own, soothing the horse, then going to the tack room where the owner worked on saddle soaping a bridle.

"Yep. He come bouncin' in here like a ball. All het up, he was. Him and the woman lit out on horses like they had their tail feathers caught in a wringer."

"Woman?" Slocum felt cold inside. How had Carrie Sinclair found Barclay before he had?

"You know the one. The old lady what found the diamond in the turkey craw. Cain't remember her name."

"Mrs. Rasmussen?"

"She's the one. Spry for a woman that old, I'd say. She rides better 'n most men."

"You act like you don't know her too well. She's from

around here. Her husband died and left her property out by the hydraulic mine.''

The stable owner scratched his head, spat, then said, ''Don't think so. Never seen her before a week or two ago. I've lived here most of my life and don't know any Rasmussen. Certainly don't know a widow woman by that name. Figured she was just another of 'em comin' into Oroville to make their fortune off them damn-fool diamonds.''

Something Carrie Sinclair had said to Slocum came back. He had wondered aloud about Mrs. Rasmussen being at the Embarcadero in San Francisco when Barclay greeted Ian Cuegant off the ship. Carrie had said that maybe the woman was visiting relatives.

Like Astin Barclay? Had the pair of them gone to San Francisco together because they knew each other? Finding a diamond in a turkey crop had resurrected Barclay's stock sales.

''Which way did Barclay and the woman ride?'' Slocum asked.

''Cain't rightly say. They bought horses and tack and lit out, just as I said. Money was good. Didn't pay attention to where they were headin'. Reckon it might be to the mine since that's all Barclay ever talked about. Damned hydraulic mine's been nothin' but trouble for this town from the day it opened.'' The man went back to cleaning and polishing the bridle.

Slocum went outside into the growing heat of the morning and looked around. Barclay and Mrs. Rasmussen were gone. The only ones left who might answer the flock of questions he had were the jeweler and Carrie Sinclair.

He set off to find them. This time he wouldn't stop until he got some answers that suited him.

18

Slocum found he didn't have to search very hard for Astin Barclay. A furor at the edge of town alerted Slocum to something unusual happening. Beside the road Barclay had set up a small table and was hastily selling more shares of stock in his land company. He looked up when he saw Slocum and turned pale. He licked his lips, then stood and stepped back from the table.

"That's all today, good people," Barclay said in a quavering voice. He looked around like a rabbit that had just spotted a coyote coming for him. Barclay couldn't find his hole to jump into. Slocum wasn't going to let him. Sitting his horse with his hand resting on his six-gun, Slocum waited for Barclay to shoo away the crowd.

The people went away grumbling at the money they had lost by not paying exorbitant rates for more shares in Barclay's Great California Land Company.

"How much are you charging now for a share in your company?" Slocum had to ask.

"Fifteen dollars. It's a good deal, Mr. Slocum. You see—"

"Shut up," Slocum said coldly. "You're not going to say a word unless it answers a question I ask. Got it?"

Barclay's head bobbed up and down like it was on a spring.

"Where's Mrs. Rasmussen, if that's even her name?"

"You know!"

"Of course I do," Slocum said. He slid from the saddle and walked to the table. Barclay had several thousand dollars scattered across the surface.

"She's my wife. The finest actress who ever trod the boards, she is," Barclay said with some pride.

"You two concocted this scheme to bilk everyone, is that it? There aren't any diamonds to be found around here, right?"

"I wouldn't say that."

"Barclay." The edge to Slocum's voice made Barclay turn even paler. "The truth. From the start."

"I, uh, it's difficult to know where to begin. My dear wife, Rita, and I found no critic willing to lavish the praise on our dramatic talents we so richly deserved."

"Astin, shut up. You don't have to tell him a damned thing!" Rita Barclay hiked up from down near the river where she had been washing clothes—and her face. Slocum remembered her as an old hag. Many of the wrinkles had been created with theatrical makeup. She looked about the same age as her husband, rather than years older.

"Ian Cuegant died. I want to find who plugged him," said Slocum. "The other two who kidnapped your husband are both dead. Who were they?"

Barclay shrugged. "Two drifters we hired for the roles of highwaymen and various kidnappers and other brigands. They should not have died. They were nothing more than innocents."

"Innocents, hell," snapped Rita Barclay. "They took our money."

"And Ian Cuegant's?"

"And Emerson's! He's in this up to his money-grasping eyebrows, the son of a bitch!" The woman shoved her husband, who cringed. "Why'd you ever get us involved with a crook like Henry Emerson?"

"But my honey, my love, he offered us so much!"

"Emerson is behind this?" Slocum felt the world spinning around—and coming into focus.

"He, along with Cuegant and the other two feckless oafs, were responsible for the fake kidnapping," Barclay admitted. "We hoped to spark interest and bring the true value of stock in the Great California Land Company to the fore."

"That worked well," Slocum said. "I found a gold pin one of the kidnappers dropped. It was Emerson's." Slocum remembered the gold head on the cane the mining magnate carried.

"He's greedy, too greedy," muttered Rita Barclay.

Slocum went on. "Cuegant was brought in to declare this a diamond find and incite the people of Oroville to buy stock in your company so you could pay Emerson a small fortune for his petered-out gold mine, is that it?" It sounded so simple, yet so many people had been involved in it. Astin Barclay and his wife, the two drifters, Ian Cuegant.

And a jeweler.

"What of the gray-haired man? The jeweler from San Francisco?" Slocum asked.

Barclay looked panicky again, and his wife turned cagey. Slocum wondered what new gold he had found in this rich vein of truth.

"Spit it out," Slocum ordered.

"What's it worth to you?" asked Mrs. Barclay. "Worth letting us ride on out?"

"With the money you stole from the people in Oroville?"

"Why not? They're as greedy a bunch as I've ever seen. 'A fool and his money are soon parted.' They've been mighty foolish."

"You'd deal Emerson out and keep the money he was supposed to get? That sounds risky to me," Slocum observed.

"We'll take our chances, Mr. Slocum," Barclay said. He licked his lips. "What about it? A deal?"

Slocum shrugged. He had no reason to take on the role of Oroville's champion. The people had let their own avarice drive them into foolish investments, even if Barclay and the others in this hoax had done a great deal to prey on that avarice.

"A deal," Slocum said. "No skin off my nose."

"Emerson's fortunes have been dwindling. There are no more gold mines, hydraulic or hardrock, for him to exploit. While creditors buzz around his head like mosquitoes hunting for a bloody banquet, he is still possessed of considerable resources."

"Enough to buy a few diamonds to salt the mine," said Rita Barclay.

"Yes, yes," Barclay hurried on. He began to appear even more nervous, as if Emerson might ride up and accuse him of traitorous acts. "I was to 'find' diamonds and flash them around. You saved the only real one I had from being stolen in San Francisco. I still owe you for that rescue, Mr. Slocum."

Slocum waved it off. "Keep talking."

"Rita was to prime the pump with a discovery by posing as a local. Ian was to come in as agent for DeBeers and make offers for the stones Gutherie appraised."

"Gutherie? The jeweler?"

"Yes," Barclay said. Again a hint of a sly look cut through the fear masking his pudgy features. "He was to announce fabulous prices. A few dollars might change hands, but mostly between us. If I paid out a thousand dollars to Rita, she could give the same money to Cuegant to buy diamonds from Gutherie."

"That's why Cuegant was so upset when I made him buy my shares in the Great California Land Company," Slocum said, grinning. "He paid five thousand and that was money taken out of the scheme."

"We tried to get you to reinvest," Rita said. "Astin ought to have offered you twice as many shares for the money, but he was too stupid to do that."

"Please, dear," Barclay said uncomfortably. "Mr. Slocum would have become suspicious if I had done that when other shares were being sold for five dollars to townspeople."

"I was already sure something fishy was going on," Slocum said. "Cuegant's reaction convinced me he was involved in it up to his neck."

Neither of the Barclays said anything. Slocum filled in the gap to keep them talking.

"You all knew one another. Actors?"

"Why, yes, all of us. We met Ian on a tour of Europe several years ago. A fine man."

"A fine, dead man," Slocum pointed out. "If you didn't kill him, what about this Gutherie? Somebody had to kill Cuegant to keep him from talking."

"Gutherie kill anyone? Absurd," said Rita. "Besides, Ian was his—" She cut off her sentence and grabbed at the money when she heard horses thundering along the road.

Slocum glanced over his shoulder. Two drunk miners were racing, both sitting backward on their horses. They whooped and hollered and somehow managed to hang on as they galloped past.

"Nothing important," Slocum said, turning back. Both Barclay and his wife were gone. He started to follow them down the embankment, then stopped when he saw them getting into a rowboat and struggling to get into the swiftly flowing river. He drew his pistol, then lowered it. They had given him enough information to convince him they had not killed Ian Cuegant.

He could track them down, trying to follow the river as it made its way across the countryside, but it hardly seemed worth it. Barclay had made off with a whale of a lot of money, but none of it was Slocum's.

Still, questions burned in his mind. Cuegant had been killed, and the gunman had wanted to put Slocum away too. That didn't set well—and Slocum knew where to find out the answer to the rest of the puzzle.

He rode to the jeweler's shop on the other side of town. It didn't surprise him to see Gutherie inside, cramming valuables into sacks as he prepared to leave town.

"Howdy, Gutherie," Slocum said from the doorway. The man jumped as if Slocum had stuck him with a needle.

"How'd you—never mind," the jeweler said. "Carrie said you were a smart one."

"Need a few more facts before I decide who killed Cuegant and tried to kill me. I'm thinking it is Emerson. He killed Cuegant to keep him from talking, and ordered Cuegant to kill me because I was an annoyance."

"Everyone's an annoyance to him," Gutherie said grimly. "What are you going to do?"

"I've figured out the land scam. All a fraud. Barclay has most of the money, and he's lit out with his wife."

"You *do* know a great deal." Gutherie closed the sack and threw it over his shoulder. "I think we'd all better join Barclay on the road before Emerson discovers what's going on. He's not a man to cross."

"He did all this to bilk money from the people of Oroville?"

"Emerson doesn't care who he steals from. The mine wasn't giving him gold any longer. He came up with the diamond hoax to milk the last drop out of the area."

"Why'd you go along with this? You *are* a jeweler, aren't you? That gold pin was your work."

"So you don't know it all." Gutherie laughed, then gasped as a bullet ripped through his heart. He sank bonelessly to the floor, dead instantly.

Slocum whipped out his six-shooter and turned. Whoever had killed Gutherie had made a fantastic shot from across the street. The slug had robbed Gutherie of his life after passing through the partially opened door. Or had the sniper been aiming for Slocum's back and missed?

Such coincidences didn't happen twice. Slocum guessed Emerson was getting rid of loose ends. And if he killed off enough people, Slocum might be the only one left to take the blame. If the townspeople got it into their heads Slocum had helped defraud them of piles of money, there wouldn't be much of a trial. He would swing from the nearest oak limb seconds after they tied the hangman's noose.

If the crowd didn't rip him apart with their bare hands. Not only would they have lost money, their dreams would have been dashed. That promise of wealth and the sorry reality of the fraud might be worse than the loss.

Slocum lit out after the gunman, but couldn't find him across the street. He stood, Colt in hand, thinking hard. A coldness settled in his gut when he realized who would be next to enter the iron sights on the murderer's rifle. Running flat out, Slocum sprinted for the boardinghouse where Carrie Sinclair stayed.

He went directly to the window of Carrie's room and peered in. She struggled to fasten a strap around a large grip.

"Carrie!" he called. She jerked around, a derringer in her hand. It looked to be the twin of the ones Ian Cuegant had carried. "Don't. Emerson's on the way. He just shot Gutherie."

Slocum wasn't sure what reaction he expected from her,

but not the one he got. She dropped the pistol and sat heavily on the bed, her stricken expression so desolate Slocum thought she was going to faint. He slid through the window and went to her.

"Gutherie was a friend, wasn't he?" Slocum said. "Like Barclay and his wife? You're an actress too?"

"He wasn't a friend, John. He was my father!"

It was Slocum's turn to be stunned. She had told him her father was a jeweler, but he had never connected her with Gutherie.

"Gutherie? What's your name?"

She turned her pasty face toward him. Her sunken bloodshot eyes showed she had been crying heavily. Lip trembling, she said, "That was his first name. Gutherie Sinclair."

"I'm sorry. I didn't know."

"That's not all you don't know," came the cold voice from the direction of the window. "Drop your six-shooter, Slocum. You've caused enough trouble."

"Emerson?"

"Who else?" The mining magnate rested the rifle on the windowsill as he worked one leg over and then tumbled into the room. "You haven't told him everything, have you, Carrie?"

"Told me what?" asked Slocum.

"Ian Cuegant was her husband."

Slocum had nothing to say. Everything fell together in one big crooked picture now. Barclay and his wife, Carrie and her husband, all out-of-work actors hired by Emerson to commit this fraud on an entire town. They fueled avarice and fanned the flames at every turn with their "discoveries" and "bargains" and "revelations."

"I should never have brought my papa into this," she said. "But it seemed so right."

"It was, it was," Emerson said. "I got rid of your husband. Just killed your father. Now it's your turn."

"I'm going to take the fall for this?" asked Slocum.

"Who else? I seem to have let Barclay and his shrew of a wife get away, but I'll find them. I suspect they have the money, don't they, Carrie? Were you supposed to meet them later and divvy *my* money, or were they dealing you out too?"

Slocum feinted to the right and caused Emerson to follow the motion. Slocum dropped to the floor and retrieved the derringer Carrie had dropped. Two weapons fired. The shot from the rifle and the one from the derringer came as one. But only one marksman was on target.

Emerson smiled and said, "You lose." Then he died.

"That was a close one," Slocum said, standing. He turned and went white-hot with anger.

Carrie Sinclair—Carrie Cuegant—had been shot in the chest between her breasts. The small red spot spread as her heart kept beating. As Slocum watched, the spurting stopped and became an ooze only because of the position of her body sprawled across the bed.

Loud cries from outside prompted Slocum to action. He placed the derringer in Carrie's still-warm fingers, then ducked out the window as the landlady burst into the room. A shriek of terror rent the air.

Slocum melted in with the crowd rushing in to see what had happened. He heard the marshal say, "Killed one another, didn't they? Clear as can be. He shot her with the rifle, she shot him with that hideout gun. Can't say why. Maybe they was lovers and had a falling-out. Surely does look like this might be the rifle what killed the jeweler too."

Slocum slipped away to let the marshal and his deputies speculate on the sudden rash of crime in their town.

Nothing but death had stalked his trail since he rode into Oroville. The two nameless drifters were both dead. Carrie, her husband, and her father—all dead. Henry Emerson had thought to be the recipient of all the money bilked from Oroville residents by the diamond hoax. Dead too.

"You leavin' town, mister?" asked the boy at the livery stable.

"Reckon so. Nothing to keep me here."

"Nothin' here at all, if you ask me. My pa says there ain't no diamonds."

"Tell your father for me that he's a smart man," Slocum said. "You mind if I borrow a shovel?"

"One's over in the corner," the boy said, puzzled by the request.

Slocum went to the back of the stall and dug up the Mason jar with the cornmeal bag inside. He set the jar on the top of the stall and tucked the rough bag into his saddlebags.

"What's that, mister?"

"About all the good that's come out of my visit to Oroville, son," Slocum said. He led his horse out into the hot sun, mounted, and rode off slowly, going past the bank where the San Francisco bankers congregated in front, undoubtedly counting on the tremendous profits they would make in diamond mining. He tipped his hat in their direction and kept riding.

He had sold part of his stock to Ian Cuegant for five thousand dollars. Slocum had sold his remaining ten thousand shares to the bankers' consortium for another dollar a share. Fifteen thousand dollars in greenbacks now rode in his saddlebags.

Let them discover Emerson's chicanery on their own. Slocum had a wad of money—and memories no amount of money could sweeten.